KB086209

문 앞에서

도서출판 아시아에서는 《바이링궐 에디션 한국 대표 소설》을 기획하여 한국의 우수한 문학을 주제별로 엄선해 국내외 독자들에게 소개합니다. 이 기획은 국내외 우수한 번역가들이 참여하여 원작의 품격을 최대한 살렸습니다. 문학을 통해 아시아의 정체성과 가치를 살피는 데 주력해 온 도서출판 아시아는 한국인의 삶을 넓고 깊게 이해하는 데 이 기획이 기여하기를 기대합니다.

Asia Publishers presents some of the very best modern Korean literature to readers worldwide through its new Korean literature series 〈Bilingual Edition Modern Korean Literature〉. We are proud and happy to offer it in the most authoritative translation by renowned translators of Korean literature. We hope that this series helps to build solid bridges between citizens of the world and Koreans through a rich in-depth understanding of Korea.

바이링궐 에디션 한국 대표 소설 053

Bi-lingual Edition Modern Korean Literature 053

Outside the Door

이동하
문 앞에서

Lee Dong-ha

ASIA
PUBLISHERS

Contents

문 앞에서

Outside the Door

아파트의 문은 잠겨 있었다. 그 철제 현관문은 견고하게 닫아 걸린 채 주인의 귀가를 완강히 거부하고 있는 것처럼 보였다. 그새 페인트칠을 다시 한 모양이다. 한 달하고도 닷새 만에 놀아온 그의 눈에는 그것이 무척 낯설게 느껴졌다. 그는 몹시 지친 상태였다. 그럴 만도 한 것이, 자그마치 천 리 길을 왔던 것이다. 얼른 문을 따고 들어가 방바닥에 길게 드러눕고 싶은 마음뿐이었다. 그는─부질없는 짓인 줄 알면서도─한 번 더 초인종을 눌러보았다. 이미 열 번도 넘게 해본 짓이다. 닫힌 문 너머에서 아주 맑고 고운 울림이 딩동딩동 몇 차례인가 울려퍼졌다. 그러나 그뿐, 안으로부터는 역시 아

The apartment door was locked. The iron front door, locked solid, seemed like it was obstinately rejecting the return of the apartment owner. The door seemed newly painted. After his long absence, one month and five days to be exact, it looked quite unfamiliar to him. He was utterly exhausted. Naturally. After all, he had traveled as far as 250 miles to come home. All he wanted was to get inside and lie completely sprawled out. He rang the doorbell again, knowing that it was useless. He had already rung it more than ten times. Beyond the closed door echoed the clear, sweet sound of the bell. However, there was no sign of life inside.

Completely dispirited, he gave up and turned

무런 인기척이 없었다.

한껏 맥이 풀린 그는 그제야 단념을 하고 천천히 돌아섰다. 그리고는 그놈의 철제문에 등을 기댄 채 대책 없이 한참을 서 있었다. 그러자니 영 난감하고, 그리고 약간 계면쩍은 기분이 들었다. 이게 무슨 꼴인가. 출발하기 전에 전화라도 해둘 걸 그랬다고, 그는 설핏 후회하는 마음이 되었다. 하지만, 남의 집을 방문하는 것도 아니잖은가. 귀가할 적마다 매번 전화질을 한다는 것도 영 객쩍은 노릇이라고 그는 생각하였다. 때문에 그는 종종 이런 낭패를 당하곤 하였다. 특히 귀가날짜가 불규칙한 경우에 그랬다. 통상 그의 귀가는—별스런 일이 없는 한—매달 마지막 주말로 정해져 있었다. 어언 10년 가까운 세월을 되풀이하나보니 이제는 식구들까지도 그렇게 길들여져버렸다. 그런데 이번은 그렇질 못하였다. 지난 주말엔 별스런 사정이 있었던 것이다. 물 건너 제주도를 3박 4일간 다녀온 졸업여행이 그것이었다. 그는 물론 인솔자의 입장으로서였는데, 똑같은 코스를 동일한 자격으로 여행한 게 이번으로 여섯 번째였다.

어쨌거나, 직장과 가정 사이에는 천 리 길이 가로놓여 있는 것이다. 어느 쪽에서 출발하든 넌덜머리나는 여정

around slowly. And he stood there, leaning against that cursed iron door, for a long while, not knowing what to do next. He felt at a loss and somewhat regretful. *What have I done! I should have called before I left!* He felt rueful. *But I was coming home, for goodness' sake, not paying a visit to someone else.* He thought it so nonsensical to call every time and let his family know that he was coming home. This self-justification had often led him into the same wretched situation, especially when his homecoming became irregular. Unless there was some unexpected turn of affairs, he usually returned home on the last weekend of every month. Having kept this schedule for some ten years, his family was now entirely accustomed to it. Nevertheless, it was different this time. Over the previous weekend, something unexpected had cropped up: he had been to Jeju Island on a three-day-four-night graduation trip. He had been, of course, the leader of the group of graduating students, for the sixth time, on exactly the same itinerary.

Anyway, there was the 250-mile distance between his home and work. Wherever he departed from, the trip was always the same: long and sickening. Even after all those trips back and forth, he

11

이기는 마찬가지였다. 그만큼 오르내렸으면 이제는 그럭저럭 내성이 붙을 법도 하건만 사정은 전혀 그렇지 못하였다. 그는 거의 언제나 대중교통—그러니까 주로 고속버스 편—을 이용해왔는데, 종점에 닿기까지는 매번 이를 갈 만큼 된통 몸살을 치르곤 하였다. 그러므로, 그에게 있어서 귀가행위는 고행에 해당하는 셈이었다. 가정이란, 밖에서 얻은 피로와 스트레스를 풀고 삶의 의욕과 활력을 재충전받는 공간 어쩌구 하는 말은, 적어도 그에게는 지극히 공허한 소리에 지나지 않았다. 되레, 그 먼 길을 오가는 것만으로도 더 지쳐빠지기 일쑤였던 것이다. 그럼에도 불구하고 굳이 집을 찾아야 하는 까닭은 무엇인가? 글쎄. 그 점에 대한 분명한 확신이 없는 채 그는 어쨌든 한 달에 대충 한 번꼴로 집을 향하여 천 리 길을 나서곤 해왔던 터이다. 특별히 발목 잡힐 일이 없는 한 매월 마지막 주의 금요일 오후에 나서서 일요일 오후에 되돌아가는—2박 3일의, 지겹고 몸살 나는 순례였다.

  닫힌 문 앞을 떠나기 전에 그는, 무겁게 들고 있던 가방을 철제문의 손잡이에다 걸어두었다. 그의 손때가 반질반질하게 묻어 있는, 그래서 훈장 관록이 만만치 않

had yet to get used to it. His means of travel was almost always public transportation, that is, the express bus where he had to endure the agony of fatigue each journey. He grit his teeth until the bus pulled into the terminal. In other words, homecoming was a sort of torture to him. What people said about home, that home was where you could escape from the fatigue and stress of the outside world and recharge yourself with a fresh supply of energy, blahblah—was nothing but a bunch of meaningless talk, at least to him. Contrary to the clichés, he felt drained of all his vital energy while going back and forth over the long distance. Why then do I come home at all? He wondered.

Without any convincing answer to that question, he had been setting out for home on the 250-mile journey roughly once every month. As far as there was nothing urgent tying him down at work, he always left for home on the last Friday afternoon of the month, only to travel back to work on Sunday afternoon. It was a sickening two-night-three-day-long pilgrimage that consumed all his energy.

Before he walked away from the locked door, he hung his heavy bag on the metal doorknob. The bag had been hand-stained to a shine and thereby

13

게 느껴질 법도 한 그런 가방이다. 하지만 속사정은 달라서, 책이라고는 찻간에서 뒤져보던 주간지가 고작으로, 온통 빨랫감만 꾸깃꾸깃 들어 앉아 있을 따름이었다. 그나마, 도무지 함부로 내놓기가 민망스러운 그런 것들이 대부분이었다. 그런데도 매번 지겹도록 무겁게 느껴지는 까닭을 잘 모르겠다고, 그는 새삼스레 한숨을 내쉬었다. 그러고는 고개를 잔뜩 꺾은 채, 그 어둠침침한 아파트 계단을 천천히 내려가기 시작하였다.

그의 아파트는 5층짜리 저층 아파트의 맨 위층이었다. 더 위로는 나름대로 멋을 낸 붉은 기와지붕이 있고, 그리고 또 그 위는 탁 트인 하늘이었다. 그 하늘과 지붕 위엔 거의 언제나 새들이 있었다. 특히 까치니 비둘기 떼가 언제나 무리지어 내려앉곤 하였다. 말하자면 그들이 유일한 위층의 주민인 셈이었다. 그 사실은 썩 기분 좋은 일이었고, 그래서 꼭대기 층까지 걸어서 오르내리는 수고를 그는 조금도 마다하지 않았다. 하긴 도무지 달갑지 않은, 또 다른 부류의 주민이 있기는 하였다. 지붕의 기왓골이나 천장의 잡다한 내장재 틈서리마다에 자리를 잡고 무섭게 번식하고 있는 바퀴벌레들이 바로 그들이었다. 그 족속들이 화장실 벽이나 부엌의 조리대

14

was likely to show his formidable dignity as a career teacher. However, the contents of the bag was a different story altogether. Other than a weekly magazine that he had thumbed through on the bus, the bag was crammed with dirty clothes to wash. Moreover, the dirty clothes themselves were mostly the things that he would have been too embarrassed to take out in front of other people. Wondering why it always felt so terribly heavy despite its trivial contents, he let out a sigh unwittingly. Then, drooping his head, he began walking down the dimly lit stairs.

His apartment was on the top floor of a five-story building. The apartment building had a red-tiled roof, beautiful in its own way against the blue expanse of the sky. Constantly present were birds both in the sky and down on the roof. Especially, magpies and pigeons frequently alighted on the roof in flocks. In a way, they were the only residents on the floor above his, which pleased him so much that he thought nothing of having to walk up to the top floor and then down from. Come to think of it, there were another, unwelcome kind of residents living in the roof as well. Cockroaches multiplied at formidable speeds either in the fur-

위 같은 곳을 유유자적 나돌아다니는 꼴을 목격하는 경우가 드물지 않았는데 그럴 때 보면 개중에는, 어찌나 크고 살이 올라 있는지 흡사 기름에 잘 튀겨놓은 번데기 같은 놈도 종종 눈에 띄었다. 그의 기분 좋은 이웃인 새들이 지붕 위에다 무시로 깔겨놓은 오물 탓이라고 아내는 곧잘 불평을 늘어놓곤 하였지만, 그러나 그는 별로 신경 쓰지 않았다.

1층까지 내려오는 사이에 아내와 마주치기를 은근히 기대하면서 그는 천천히, 근력이 시원찮은 노인네처럼 아주 느릿느릿 걸어서 계단을 다 내려왔다. 그러나 그 기대는 역시 헛된 것이었다. 대신 그의 눈에 띈 것은 현관 벽에 나란히 붙어 있는 편지함이었다. 열 개의 함 중 유독 503호에 우편물이 잔뜩 들어 있었다. 그는 그것들을 몽땅 뽑아내어가지고 선 채로 하나하나 점검해보았다. 〈번지 내 투입〉이라 찍힌 홍보지가 몇 종—요즘 들어 특히 이런 종류의 우편물이 부쩍 늘어가는 추세다. 최근에 창간된 지역 신문 한 장—비매품이다. 전화 요금 고지서—얼핏 보아 이달에도 적지 않은 액수다. 아파트 관리비 통지서, 뉴스위크지, 대입 수험지, 그리고 모 사회봉사단체와 증권사 두어 군데서 보내온 유인물

rows of the roof tiles or in the gaps and crevices in the various ceiling-finishing materials. He had, more often than not, witnessed the bugs crawling freely on the bathroom walls or kitchen table, some of which were so big and fat that they looked like those shiny, deep-fried pupas. His wife repeatedly complained that it was the droppings of the birds, their otherwise good neighbors, that attracted cockroaches to the roof, but he never bothered himself with the issue.

Hoping to run into his wife on the way, he walked down the stairs very slowly to the ground floor like a tottering old man, only to get disappointed once more. What caught his eyes, instead of his wife, at the foot of the stairs was the rows of mailboxes attached to the wall of the entry hall. Among the ten boxes there, only the one belonging to Apartment 503 was stuffed with mail. He took all of the mail out of the box and checked one by one. Some were fliers with "Delivery at Address" stamped on them--increasing numbers of which found their way in the mailbox recently. Next was a not-for-sale local newspaper that had just been launched, followed by the phone bill—which was, even at a quick glance, not at all a small amount

등등…… 가정의 일상사를 잠시 들여다본 기분이어서 그로서는 그다지 유쾌하지 못하였다. 그런 것들은 아마도 아내나 아이들의 삶과 더 많이 관계되리라. 하지만 자신에게는 대체로 생소한 것이었으므로 그는 그것들을 다시 제자리에다 아무렇게나 쑤셔박아두었다. 그리고는 손을 털고 나서 1층 현관을 나섰다. 흘낏 시계를 들여다보았다. 오후 5시가 조금 지난 시각이었다.

아내가 슈퍼에 갔을지도 모른다는 생각이 제일 먼저 그의 머리에 떠올랐다. 도시 사람, 특히 아파트 단지에 사는 사람들은 생필품의 거의 대부분을 그런 곳에서 공급받고 있으므로 그 생각은 썩 그럴싸하게 느껴졌다. 더군나나 수부들은 이제 저녁상을 걱정해야 할 시간이다. 언젠가도 이런 낭패 끝에 단지 안 슈퍼에서 아내와 극적으로(?) 조우한 바가 있었던 것이다. 그때 아내는, 두 팔이 늘어지게 들고 나오던 비닐 꾸러미 중 하나를 그에게 넘겨주면서 불평을 했었다. 돈 쓰는 일도 힘들다구요. 맨날 식구들 거둬 멕이는 것만도 중노동이에요……

평소 아내가 드나들던 슈퍼는 세 곳이었다. 그들이 속

this month again, the statement of apartment maintenance fee payments, an issue of *Newsweek*, a set of practice tests for the college entrance examination, some printed materials from a volunteer social work organization and a couple of stock companies, and so forth. He felt that he had just peered into his family's everyday life, which didn't cheer him up at all. Those aspects of life would probably have been more meaningful to his wife and children; but they were mostly unfamiliar to him. He crammed the great wad back into the mailbox carelessly. After brushing dust off his hands, he walked out of the entry hall on the ground floor. He took a glance at his watch. It was about half past five in the afternoon.

Just then, it suddenly occurred to him that his wife might be shopping at a supermarket. City dwellers, especially those living in apartment complexes, have most of their daily necessities supplied by neighborhood supermarkets, which made his hope of finding his wife in one of the nearby grocery stores more plausible. Moreover, it was the time of day when housewives would usually busy themselves worrying about dinner for their families. He had once been in a similar fix and in the end,

해 있는 7단지 슈퍼와, 그리고 이웃한 6, 8단지 슈퍼가 그것이었다. 그는 대단한 기대를 걸고 세 군데를 차례로 순방하였다. 하지만 극적인 상봉은 이루어지지 않았다. 허전한 노릇이었다. 그 허전함 때문에 그는 내처 5, 6단지 사이의 굴다리시장까지 좇아가 기웃거렸다. 집에 머물 때면 더러, 아내의 장바구니를 들어주기 위해 따라나오곤 하던 곳—어물전 앞에서는 생고등어를 사라고 아내의 옆구리를 집적거렸다가 무안을 당하기도 하고, 또 옛날 생각 때문에 잠시 나이며 주제를 잊은 채 풀빵을 쩝쩝 사 먹기도 하던 곳이었다. 때가 때이니만치 그 좁은 거리는 장보러 나온 아낙네들로 한창 복작대는 판이었다. 그들 사이를 헤치고 다니기가 좀 민망스러울 시경이었다. 그럼에도 불구하고 그는 이 끝에서 저쪽 끝까지 막무가내로 뚫고 간 다음, 거기서 다시 온 길을 되짚어 샅샅이 뒤졌지만 결과는 역시 허무하였다. 너무 일방적인 기대였음을, 그는 비로소 깨닫는 기분이 되었다. 얼굴이 홧홧하게 달아올랐다.

다리가 꽤나 팍팍하였다. 이럭저럭 한 시간 가까이 헤매고 다닌 꼴이었다. 등때기가 축축하게 젖어버렸다. 그는 어깨를 축 늘어뜨린 채 스적스적 걸어갔다. 허리

had a "dramatic" encounter with his wife in a supermarket in the apartment complex. At the time,
his wife had handed him one of the heavy plastic
bags she was carrying and had complained:
"Spending money is hard, too. Feeding the family
every day, that alone is a hard labor."

There were three supermarkets where his wife
often shopped: the one in the 7th Complex that his
apartment building belonged to and the other two
in the 6th and 8th Complexes, respectively. In great
hopes, he visited the three supermarkets one after
another. Nevertheless, the expected "dramatic" encounter didn't take place. He felt deflated, which
somehow compelled him to go farther to the Tun-
nel Market located in between the 5th and the 6th
Complex. On the days he stayed home, he would
follow his wife to this outdoor market every now
and then to help her carry the shopping baskets.
He remembered being put to shame in front of the
fishmonger's after nudging his wife in the ribs to
make her buy fresh mackerel, and then eating
cheap waffles stuffed with sweet bean paste, remi-
niscent of his childhood, for a moment forgetting
completely how old or what he was. Because of
the time of day, the narrow road was crowded with

를 꺼부정하게 굽힌 채 팔다리를 앞뒤로 흐느적거리는 그런 걸음걸이였다. 아내가 곁에 있었다면 또 한 소리 얻어들었으리라. 그 걸음걸이는 아내가 몹시 싫어하는, 그의 나쁜 버릇 중 하나였기 때문이다. 당신 걸음걸이가 그게 뭐예요? 아예 날더러 업고 가자고 하세요. 그 편이 남 보기에도 좋을 것 같수…… 하지만 지금은 아내의 지청구가 아쉬웠다. 그러자 문득, 그새 아내가 돌아왔을지도 모른다는 생각이 불쑥 들었다. 그것은 단순한 기대 수준을 넘어서 어느새 확신 비슷한 것이 되어버렸다. 7단지로 들어서자 저만치 뒤편으로 그의 아파트 베란다가 비스듬히 보였다. 하지만 결코 서두르고 싶은 마음은 없었다.

그는 계단을 천천히 올라갔다. 4층과 5층의 중간 지점에서 그는 일단 발을 멈추고 서서 고개를 쳐들었다. 먼저 눈에 띈 것은 가방이었다. 그 물건이 손잡이에 그대로 걸려 있었다. 아내가 돌아오지 않았다는, 분명한 징표였다. 실망이 클 법한데도 별로였다. 어쩌면 이번 역시 그닥 기대를 두지 않았던 것인지도 모를 노릇이었다. 단지 그의 어깨가 좀 더 처졌을 따름이었다.

굳이 꼭대기까지 올라갈 이유가 없었다. 그 자리에서

the shopping housewives. He felt a bit embarrassed elbowing his way through the crowd. Nevertheless, he pushed on from one end of the road to the other, and back, combing every inch of the market, to no avail. He then realized that his expectations were entirely one-sided. He felt his cheeks burn with shame.

His legs hurt quite a bit. He had been walking for almost an hour. His back felt wet in a sweat. He slouched along with his arms swaying limply by his sides. It was his way of walking, leaning forward, moving his arms and legs about limply. If his wife had been there with him, he would have heard her nagging. It was one of his habits his wife hated so much. "Why on earth do you walk like that? You might as well ask me to carry you on my back. That'll look better to other people." Nevertheless, he missed his wife's grumbling now. All of a sudden, a thought flashed across his mind: his wife might have been back home already. Then the thought quickly transformed itself from a simple expectation into a sort of conviction. Once he entered the 7th Complex, he could see the verandah of his apartment diagonally. However, he didn't want to hurry at all.

그대로 돌아서려다가 그는 문득 엉뚱한 환영을 보았다. 무척 낯익은 얼굴 하나가 머리 위 허공에서 불쑥 나타나더니 그를 빤히 내려다보았던 것이다. 아주 순간적으로 섬뜩한 느낌이 들었던 까닭은 무엇보다, 그것이 바로 자기 자신의 모습이란 자각 때문이었다. 동남향으로 앉은 건물이어서 저녁 무렵엔 계단실이 다소 어둡다고는 해도, 그러나 사람의 얼굴조차 못 알아볼 정도는 아니었다. 바로 코앞에서 맞바라보고 있는 그 얼굴은 좀 더 늙고 조금 더 초췌해 보이기는 해도 영락없는 자신의 몰골이던 것이다. 몹시 귀에 익은, 탁하고 어눌하고 기어드는 듯한, 그 특유의 목소리가 그 순간 들려오지 않았다면 그는 아마도 기절해 나자빠졌거나 아니면 혼비백산하여 층계를 굴러내렸을 것이었다.

「보래이…… 넴이 니…… 아이가?」

그 한마디로 족하였다. 단번에 상대를 알아본 그는 서둘러 계단을 올라갔다. 역시 그랬다. 천만뜻밖에도 아버지가 거기, 잠긴 문 앞에 엉거주춤하게 서 있었다.「아부지가 어쩐 일이세요?」

「올라오능 거 보이께네 넴이 니지 싶으더라.」

종남이의 〈남〉이를 아버지는 늘 〈넴〉이라고 발음하

He walked up the stairs slowly. At the landing between the fourth and fifth floor, he came to a halt and raised his head. The first thing he saw was his bag—still hanging on the doorknob. It was a clear sign that his wife hadn't returned. It could have been a big letdown for him, but in fact, it wasn't. Perhaps, he hadn't had so high expectations as he would have liked. His shoulders drooped a bit further; that was all.

There was no need to go up to the fifth floor. As he was about to turn around, he saw something completely unexpected. A very familiar face appeared in midair above his head and stared down at him. He felt chills going down his spine when he realized that it was his own face he was seeing. The building was built to face southeast, so it got somewhat dark inside at dusk, but not to the point that people couldn't recognize one another. The face, looking straight at him at close range, appearing to be a bit older and more haggard than his; nevertheless, it was unmistakably his face. If, at the moment, he hadn't heard the familiar voice— thick, inarticulate, and faint, he would have fainted away or fell down the stairs, scared out of his wits.

"Look here...aren't you...Naem-i?"

였다. 그의 기억이 미치는 한 아득한 옛날부터 그래왔다. 그 탓일까? 아버지로부터 그렇게 불리기만 하면 그는 금세 마음이 어려지는 것이었다. 냄이—그것은 때로 깊은 울림 같은 것을 불러일으키는 이름이었다.

「어쩐 일이세요 아버지?」

그는 같은 물음을 되풀이하였다. 그밖에 다른 말은 생각나지 않았다. 이 뜻밖의 해후가 조금은 감격스러웠던 것이다.

「기냥 바람이나 쐴라고 안 나섰더나. 니 안사람, 안에 없능갑제?」

「예, 잠시 집을 비운 모양입니다. 아부지는 언제 오신 거지요?」

「아까 안 왔더나.」

여전히 손잡이에 걸려 있는 가방을 가리키며 노인이 말하였다.

「아까 참에 왔을 때는 없디 요분에 와보이꺼네 저 물건이 떡 안 걸렸나. 그래, 이기 우예 된 기고 싶어서 내 한참 궁리하던 중이다……」

노인은 그러면서 허허 웃었다. 목젖이 보일 만큼 입을 벌리고 소리를 크게 내어 웃는, 특유의 웃음이었다. 그

That was good enough. He recognized the man right away and rushed up the stairs. He was right. To his great surprise, his father was standing awkwardly there in front of the locked door.

"Father! What are you doing here?"

"I had a feeling that it was you, Naem-i, coming up the stairs."

His father always called him by the second syllable of his name, Jong-nam, pronouncing it Naem instead of Nam. From as far back as he could remember, his father had been calling him Naem-i. Perhaps, that's why he felt as if he were turning into a child whenever his father called him by the name. Naem-i, it was a sound that sometimes produced a profound resonance within him.

"What are you doing here, Father?"

He repeated the question. He couldn't think of anything else to say. He was a bit touched by the unexpected encounter.

"I left home just to get some fresh air. Your wife, she isn't home, is she?"

"No, she isn't. It seems she's just stepped out. When did you arrive, Father?"

"A while ago."

The old man pointed at the bag still hanging on

도 맥없이 따라 웃었다. 부전자전이라며 그의 아내가, 어쩌면 그렇게나 속없는 웃음들일까 하고 곧잘 흉보곤 하던, 족보에 있는 바로 그 웃음이었다. 그로서는 참 오랜만에 마음이 즐거워졌다.

「그래서요?」

「니한테도 열쇠가 없능 기 분명타 싶더라.」

노인은 또 한차례 예의 웃음을 보인 다음 덧붙였다. 「니, 안사람 찾아갔지러? 어데 마실 간 기가?」

「마실요?」

되묻고 나서 그도 또 웃었다. 그럴지도 모른다. 아내의 외출을 예스럽게 말하자면 마실 간 꼴일 것이다. 아마도, 일상의 울타리를 벗어나 아주 먼 나들이를 한 것은 아닐 터이므로. 하지만 이 거대한 아파트촌에도 마실 갈 만한 이웃들이 있었던가? 새삼스레 아내의 일상이 그는 궁금해졌다.

그러자 문득 한 가지 생각이 떠올랐다. 옳거니! 그는 마음속으로 쾌재를 올렸다. 아내가 어쩌면 가 있을 법한 또 다른 장소가 생각났던 것이다. 그것은 슈퍼도 시장바닥도 아닌 제삼의 장소—바로 교회였다. 철제 문짝 위 눈높이쯤 되는 곳에 그 교회의 명패가 붙어 있었다.

the doorknob.

"When I first arrived, there was nothing on the knob. But then I came back and found that thing hanging there. So, I've been wondering for some time what's that all about."

The old man laughed, in the way typical of him: loudly, with his mouth open so wide that you could see his uvula. He couldn't help laughing along. It was the laugh that ran in the family, which his wife often picked on for, saying, "Like father, like son! Such innocent laughter!" As for him, he felt happy for the first time in a long while.

"So, what did you think it was?"

"I figured that you didn't have the key, either."

The old man laughed his usual laugh once more and added, "You went out to look for your wife, didn't you? You think she's out on a visit for a chat?"

"A visit for a chat?"

He laughed, too. 'Perhaps, Father guessed it right. She can be out on a visit for a chat, to use an old expression. She wouldn't have gone far away, though, beyond the scope of her daily life. But then, does she have neighbors close enough to visit in this huge apartment complex?' Suddenly, he

그것은 얇은 알루미늄판에 특수인쇄처리를 한 것으로 교회 이름 담임목사 이름 그리고 주소와 몇 개의 전화번호 따위가 박혀 있었다. 평소 무심히 보아 오던 것이었다. 그래, 전화를 해보자, 하고 그는 작정하였다.

공중전화는 단지 진입로 쪽에 있었다. 그는 잠시 주저하였다. 옆집 문도 굳게 닫혀 있었다. 이 집도 비었을까? 그거야 벨을 눌러보면 알 일이다. 하지만 전화 빌리는 일을 그는 포기하였다. 몇 달이 가도 서로 얼굴 한 번 부딪칠 기회가 드문 이웃들이었다.

「이대로 잠깐 기다리세요. 요 앞에 가서 전화 한 통 해보게요. 잠깐이면 됩니다.」

그는 노인을 그 자리에 세워둔 채 계단을 빠르게 내려갔다. 그리고는 공중전화가 있는 단지 입구 쪽을 향하여 열나게 뛰어갔다. 공팔사칠 공팔사칠…… 입 속으로는 연방 전화번호를 뇌면서. 다행히 국번은 같았으므로 외는 수고가 한결 덜어졌다. 그러자 참 요상하게도 또다시 낙관적인 기분이 들었다. 아내가 틀림없이 교회에 있으리라고 믿어지는 것이었다. 아내의 행동반경이야 뻔하지 않은가. 그야말로 뛰어봤자지 뭐! 그는 생각에 열중하였다. 평소에도 시장보다 교회 출입이 더

felt curious about his wife's everyday life.

Just then, a thought entered his mind. 'That's it!' He yelled for joy inside. He had just thought of another place where his wife was likely to be. Neither a supermarket nor an outdoor market, it was the church itself. There was a nameplate of a church attached to the locked door at the level of his eyes. It was a thin aluminum plate with the name of the church, the name of the minister in charge, the address of the church, and several telephone numbers written on it using a special printing method. He had known it was there but never thought much of it. Yes, I'm going to call the church, he told himself resolutely.

He knew the public phones were near the entrance to the apartment complex. He hesitated for a moment. He saw the door to the apartment next to his firmly closed. Was that apartment also empty? All he had to do was ring the bell and see if anybody answered the door. However, he gave up on borrowing his neighbor's phone. He hardly ran into the next-door neighbors; sometimes, he didn't even catch a glimpse of their faces for months.

"Wait here for a minute, please. I'll go over there and make a phone call. It won't take long."

잦았던 아내였다. 주일날이야 말할 것도 없고, 평일에도 출입이 뻔질났던 것이다. 삼일예배, 구역예배, 전도훈련, 제자훈련, 구역장모임, 여전도회모임, 새벽기도회, 금요철야기도회, 전도대회, 봉사활동, 교우경조사참례 등등…… 그래서 아내는 늘 바쁘고, 그리고 늘 조금씩 지쳐 있게 마련이던 것이다. 그것을 극성스럽다고 표현하는 사람도 적지 않다는 것을 그는 잘 알고 있었다. 그러나 그 자신은 꼭이 그렇게까지 생각하지는 않았다. 그는 단지, 게으른 사람은 천당 가는 꿈조차 꿀 일이 못 된다고만 여기고 있을 따름이었다. 그리고 자기자신은 누구 못지않게 게으른 사람이라고 진작에 단정한 바 있었다. 당신, 믿는 일을 그렇게 게을리해가지고 나중에 어쩔려구 그래요? 언젠가 아내가 하던 말을 불쑥 떠올리고 경황 중에도 그는 히물히물 웃었다. 누군 하늘나라에 가서 그랬답디다. 천성문 앞을 기웃기웃하면서, 나 아무개 집사 좀 만나게 해주시오, 그 여자가 바로 내 아내요, 라고……

아내는, 그러나 교회에도 없었다. 거의 확신에 가까웠던 기대가 허물어지고 말았음에도 불구하고, 하지만 그는, 이 또한 요상하게도 이번 역시 심상한 느낌이었다.

He left the old man standing there and rushed down the stairs. Then he ran as fast as he could towards the entrance to the complex where the public phone booths were, repeating the phone number to himself, "Zero-eight-four-seven. Zero-eight-four-seven." Fortunately the telephone exchange number was the same as his, making it easier to remember the whole thing. Strangely, however, he felt optimism growing inside himself, again. He found himself firmly believing that his wife was at the church. The radius of her movements was so obvious, wasn't it? Run as she might, she can't get too far. He tried to stay focused. Ordinarily, his wife went to church more frequently than to the markets. Even on weekdays, not to mention Sundays, she went to church often enough: Wednesday evening service, area worship, evangelical training, disciple training, area heads meeting, lady preachers meeting, early morning prayer, Friday vigils, the grand meeting of evangelism, volunteer activities, weddings and funerals of church families and so forth. So, his wife was always busy and a little tired. He was aware that not a few people talked about her as being overeager. He, however, didn't exactly agree with them. Rath-

아내가 이런 시간에 꼭이 거기에 있어야만 당연하달 수야 없지. 아무렴. 그는 혼자 중얼거리면서, 갔던 길을 다시 되돌아왔다.

다시 5층까지의 계단을 오르자니 숨이 찼다. 이게 몇 번째인가? 그는 코너마다 발길을 멈추고 잠깐씩 서 있었다. 어차피, 아내가 제 스스로 나타나줄 때까지 시간을 뭉개야 한다. 서둘 이유란 조금도 없다고 생각하였다. 그래도 5층 맨 윗 계단을 밟고 올라서려니 역시 숨이 찼다. 내일이면 쉰이다. 그리고 그 쉰 살의 나이가 헛것이 아니다─그는 문득 그런 생각을 하였다. 그러자 고희를 엊그제 넘긴 아버지의 모습이 그제야 예사롭게 느껴지지 않았다.

「그래, 우예 됐노?」

닫힌 문 앞에서 엉거주춤하게 서 있던 노인이 물었다. 「그래, 몬 찾았나? 딴 데 해볼 데도 없고? 나간 김에 대강 다 해볼 꺼로……」

그는 풀썩 웃고 나서 대답하였다. 「곧 오겠지요 뭐. 멀리 나간 건 아닐 거예요. 그 사람, 갈 데도 별루 없어요. 안방 미장원 같은 데서 머리나 볶고 있는 건 아닌지 모르겠네요. 그러자면 시간께나 걸리기두 하겠지요. 예편

er, he was of the opinion that lazy people could never even dream of going to Heaven. And he had known from earlier on that when it came to laziness, he was second to none. "You're neglecting your faith too much. What'll become of you later?" Reminding himself of his wife's warning, he couldn't help grinning, despite the scrape he was in: "I heard of a man who went to the Heavenly gates. He snooped around at the front of the gates. He pleaded, 'Please, let me see Deaconess So-and-so in there. She's my wife.'"

Unfortunately, however, his wife wasn't at the church, either. Although his expectations, which had been close to certain this time, turned out to be a false hope, he, curiously enough, once more took it matter-of-factly. "Why should she be there at this time of day? Why should she, indeed?" He muttered to himself on his way back.

Climbing the stairs up to the fifth floor, he felt short of breath. How many times had he done this? He made a brief stop at every landing. "I need to kill time anyway until she shows up. Absolutely no reason to hurry," he thought. Even with the frequent rest, he was panting hard when he reached the fifth floor. 'I'm turning fifty soon,' he suddenly

네들이란…… 젤루 흔한 게 시간이니까…… 아까운
줄을 알아야지요……」

「하모, 그래야제.」노인도 웃고 있었다.

「어데 마실 안 갔겠나. 그라이 결국에는 올 꺼 아이가.
내는 개안타. 쪼매 더 기대리보자.」

「어디 나가서 앉을자리라도 찾아보십시다.」

아들이 먼저 돌아섰고, 그 뒤를 줄레줄레 따르면서 그
의 늙은 아버지가 맞장구를 치고 있었다.「오야오야, 그
러자카이.」

그러면서 두 부자는 의좋게 1층 현관을 나섰다.

어린이놀이터를 앞에 하고 벤치가 드문드문 놓여 있
었나. 내여섯 살짜리 사내아이 하나가 그네에 매달려
있을 뿐 그 일대는 조용하였다. 두 부자는 벤치 하나를
차지하고 앉았다. 머리 위로는 등넝쿨이 제법 어우러지
고 있었다. 마침 바람기도 있어서 기분이 한결 상쾌해
졌다. 그놈의 을씨년스런 5층 계단과, 닫아 걸린 철제문
은 생각하기조차 싫었다. 그깐 놈의 것, 영원히 열리지
않는대도 아쉬울 거 없다, 굳이 따고 들어간다고 해서
무슨 대수냐! 오히려 이쪽이 한결 마음 편한 것을……

felt his age. Only then did it come home to him that his father was over seventy.

"Well, how did it go?"

The old man asked him, standing awkwardly in front of the closed door: "You didn't find her? Isn't there any place else you could call? While you were out, you should've called all the other places..."

He gave a short laugh and replied, "Well, she'll be back soon. She's probably somewhere nearby. She's few places to go. She may be getting her hair permed at some place like a living-room beauty shop. That'll take a while. Housewives! Time's the only thing they have plenty of. They should learn the value of time."

"Of course, they should." The old man was also laughing.

"She's probably visiting someone. If so, she'll be back sooner or later, won't she? Don't worry about me. Let's wait a little bit longer."

"Shall we go outside and have a sit somewhere?"

The son turned around first and his old father followed him, chiming in, "Yes, yes, of course."

The father and son walked out of the entry hall on the ground floor in friendly spirits.

마치, 아주 먼 길을 걷다가 잠시 다리를 뻗고 쉬는 것 같은 느낌이 들었다. 아파트 건물의 터진 쨈으로 1단지 너머 우뚝 솟아 있는 관악산 저녁 풍광이 더할 나위 없이 부드럽고 넉넉한 느낌을 주었다. 기상대와 송신탑이 있는 꼭대기 위로 붉은 일몰을 헤치며 여객기 한 대가 천천히 사라져 갔다.

「아까도 내 여게 안 있었더나.」

노인이 먼저 입을 뗐고, 그가 놀라 되물었다.

「그러세요? 그럼 진작에 오신 거군요?」

「얼추 서너 시간은 되지 싶으다.」

「아니, 한낮에 오신 거네요. 그러면, 점심은요?」

「오다 찻간에서 묵었다.」

「기차 말입니까?」

「하모, 통일호 타고 안 왔나.」

아들은 입을 다물었다. 대구서 서울까지―그 먼 길을 통일호로 왔노라는 얘기였다. 이름만은 썩 그럴싸한 그놈의 통일호란 왕년의 완행열차를 뜻하고 있음을 그는 너무나 익히 알고 있는 터였다. 남대문시장 뒷골목처럼 붐비고 냄새나는 속에서 점심까지 잘 자셨노라는 얘기였던 것이다. 그의 말투는 좀 퉁명스러워졌다.

They found some benches, far apart from one another, facing the playground. It was quiet around, with only one boy who was maybe five or six years old on one of the swings. The father and son sat down on one of the benches. The wisteria vines overhead were quite thick. There was even a pleasant breeze; it seemed to lift their spirits. He didn't even want to think about the gloomy stair-cases and the locked iron door. That stupid thing! Let it stay locked forever, and I've got nothing to lose. Even if it managed to open, what would be so great about that? It was more relaxing to sit out here. He felt as if he were finally enjoying a respite, his feet stretched out, after having walked a very long distance. Between the apartment buildings, he saw the evening scenery of Mt. Gwanak, in the best of its gentleness and generosity, looming beyond the 1st Complex. A passenger plane appeared above the weather observatory and transmitting tower, and flew away across the crimson sunset sky.

"I was here earlier too," the old man said.

"You were? You must have arrived much earlier, then?" surprised, the son asked.

"About three or four hours ago, I guess."

「아부지는 어째서 매양 그놈의 통일홉니까? 새마을
이나 무궁화는 없구요? 아부지는 아직도 달구에 사신
다니까……」

달구란 대구의 옛 이름이다. 노인은 소리를 내어 웃었
다. 예의 속 좋은 웃음이었다.

「내사 머 천하에 바쁠 일이 있나 어데, 완행 타고 천천
히 오면서 이런 사람 저런 사람하고 시상 얘기도 하고
그라이꺼네 좋더마는…… 하낫도 안 불편타카이.」

「아부지도 참…… 그것도 근력 좋으실 때 얘기라구
요. 그러다가 찻간에서 무슨 탈이라도 나 보세요. 어떡
헐 거예요? 꼼짝없이 생고생 하시지 뭐.」

「탈은 무신 탈! 내사 안죽 끄떡없다.」

그러나 말과는 달리 노인의 목소리엔 기력이 없었다.

「담에 오실 때는 미리 연락주세요. 안방에 매인 전화,
번호만 돌리면 될 텐데 그게 어려우세요? 그러면 새마
을 표 끊어서 부쳐드리도록 하겠습니다. 꼭 그렇게 하
세요.」

「머로 그래! 개안타, 신경 쓰지 마라.」

노인은 머리를 완강하게 내젓기까지 하였다. 그는 새
삼스레 아버지의 행색을 살펴보는 마음이 되었다.

"Really? That means you arrived around noon. What about lunch?"

"I ate on the way."

"You mean, on the train?"

"Of course, I took the Unification Line."

The son fell silent. From Daegu to Seoul—his father had traveled such a long distance on the Unification Line train. He knew only too well that the Unification Line, despite its grand name, was actually a slow train of long past. His father was saying that he had had a nice lunch on the train, crowded and smelly like in the back alleys of the Namdaemun Market. His tone turned grouchy.

"Why do you always take the Unification Line? What about New Village Line or Rose of Sharon Line? Father, you're still living in Dalgu..."

Dalgu was the old name of Daegu. The old man laughed loudly. It was that old harmless laughter of his.

"I'm not busy with anything. I enjoy riding the slow train, talking with others about the world. There's nothing uncomfortable about it."

"Father, please... That's good as long as you stay strong. What if something bad happens to you on the train. What are you gonna do? You'll have no

41

그랬다. 아버지는 여전한 모습이셨다. 꺼부정하게 굽고 비쩍 마른 체격이 우선 그랬고, 다듬지 않아 지저분한 턱수염과 한 모숨도 채 남지 않은 백발이 그랬고, 또 무엇보다 초라한 그 입성이 그랬다. 헐렁하게 걸치고 있는 남방은 노인네에겐 도무지 어울리지 않는 문양으로 온통 어지러웠는데 그나마 물이 바래고 천이 날긋날긋해 보였다. 바지는 여기저기 얼룩이 지고, 무릎께가 불쑥 튀어나와 있었다. 게다가 아랫단을 두어 번 걷어 올린 것으로 보아 바짓가랑이가 턱없이 긴 모양이었다. 요컨대, 아무리 철이 그렇다고는 해도 모처럼의 서울 나들이치고는 도무지 걸맞지 않은 차림새인 것만은 분명하였다. 흡사, 의지가지없는 떠돌이 노인네 행색이라고나 해야 할 판이었다.

그는 은연중에 한숨을 내뱉었다. 기회 있을 때마다 지적하고 간곡히 당부 드렸음에도 불구하고 당신은 늘 그런 모습이셨다. 당신은 그게 편타는 주장이었다. 뿐더러, 굳이 체면이나 위신 같은 것을 새삼스럽게 챙겨야 할 신분도 아니라는 것이었다. 「되는 대로 게오 밥이나 끓이고 살아온 한평생인데 인자 와가주고 네꾸다이 양복 걸친들 머할 끼고. 내사 마 벨볼일 없는 늙은잉 기라.

choice but to suffer it all through the ride."

"What bad thing'll happen to me? I'm as healthy as ever."

Despite his confident words, the old man's voice was feeble.

"Next time, please let us know in advance. The phone's in your master bedroom. All you have to do is dial the number. How difficult can it be? Then I'll get a New Village Line ticket and send it to you. Please, promise me you'll do it."

"What for? I'm fine as ever. Never you mind!"

The old man even shook his head stubbornly. He felt bound to get a good look at his father's appearance.

Of course! His father looked the same as ever. First of all, his stooped, lean physique was the same. His untrimmed beard and unkempt, sparse white hair was the same. Most of all, his shabby outfit was exactly the same. His loose-fitting aloha shirt was of a dizzily intricate pattern that didn't become the old man at all, and they were worn and discolored at that. His pants were stained here and there, his knees protruding. The legs were folded up a couple of times—they were much too long for him. In short, it was definitely not an outfit one

우리끼리 하는 말로, 옛고짜 고물이요 갈거짜 거물 아이가.」그러고는 저 속 좋은 웃음으로 얼버무리고 마는 것이었다.

그래도 아들 체면이라는 게 있단 말입니다, 하고 때로는 강변하고 싶은 그였다. 아버님은 그게 편하실지 모르지만 저로서는 이웃들 대하기가 민망하다구요. 그래도 명색이 선생 아닙니까. 남을 가르치는 신분 아니냐구요. 그러나, 그는 물론 그렇게 말한 적이 없었다. 매번 마음속으로만 끙끙 앓고 마는 것이었다. 언젠가 한번은 노인이 그런 모습을 한 채 그의 직장으로 불쑥 찾아온 적도 있었다. 그러나 그는 그때도 속으로만 앓고 말았다. 천성이 그렇게 타고난 분이었다. 아니, 평생을 가난 속에서 그렇게 살아온 분이기도 하였다. 남루는 곧 당신의 생리였다. 속된 말로 하자면, 이제 와서 억지로 때 빼고 광내려고 하는 쪽이 오히려 속된 것인지도 모를 일이었다.

노인 곁에는 비닐백이 하나 놓여 있었다. 그것은 노인이 항용 끼고 다니는 물건으로서, 그 낡은 정도며 속이 빈 듯 쭈그러져 있는 모양 하며, 한눈에도 주인을 아주 잘 닮아 있었다. 쓰레기통에 내던져둔들 아무도 집어가

would choose for a rare trip to Seoul, even with the season being what it was. He looked as if he were a helpless old drifter.

He let out a sigh, unwittingly. Though he took every opportunity to point out his father's clothes and to plead with him, his father always dressed himself that way. The old man insisted that he preferred comfortable clothes. Moreover, the old man continued, he had never been and was certainly not in the position where he needed to go to the trouble of saving his face or dignity.

"I've lived all my life barely feeding myself and family. What's the point of wearing suits and neckties at this point in my life? I'm just an old man, nobody important. As we old men put it, I'm an old thing, a bygone thing." His father folded over with that old harmless laughter.

"But, I need to think about my reputation!" He sometimes had an urge to put his foot down about it all. "Father, you may feel comfortable that way, but as for myself, I feel embarrassed to face my neighbors. I'm a so-called teacher, aren't I? Aren't I in a position to teach people?"

Of course, he had never said this out loud. Each time, he'd only ended up struggling to keep it sup-

지 않으리라고 생각되었다. 그는 눈을 들어 노인의 얼굴을 바라보았다. 그러자 비로소, 이마의 상처가 눈에 띄었다.

「아니, 이마는 왜 이래요?」 그는 놀라 소리쳤다.

「아이다, 삘꺼 아이다.」 노인이 손을 내저었다.

「가만 계세요.」

그는 바싹 다가앉아 상처 자리를 들여다보았다. 무슨 막대기 같은 것에 긁힌 듯싶었다. 이마에서부터 정수리까지 훤히 벗어진 머리라 상처가 유독 드러나 보였다. 이마 정중앙에서 오른쪽으로 약간 비켜 손가락 두 마디 정도의 길이로 죽 그어진 생채기가 노인의 인상을 한층 더 초라하게 만들어서 그로 하여금 불현듯 연민의 감정에 빠져들게 하였다. 아마도 다친 지 몇 시간 되지 않는 듯 상처에선 아직도 피가 삐죽이 내비치고 있었다. 그러고 보니 안경알도 온전치 못하였다. 무엇에다 된통 얼굴을 들이받은 게 분명하였다.

「어쩌다가 이랬지요? 안경 깨진 거 보니까 아주 큰일 날 뻔하셨구만요! 어디서 이랬지요?」

거푸 물으면서 그는 어깨를 축 늘어뜨렸다. 그렇게 낙심이 될 수가 없었다.

pressed. The old man had once visited him at work unannounced in his usual set of clothes. Even then, he didn't say anything, although he'd still suffered greatly inside. The old man had been born that way. And he'd also lived his whole life that way. In poverty. Shabbiness was a part of his nature. To use a common phrase, "scrubbing dirt off and rubbing on polish" at any cost, at this point, might have been a baser thing to do.

There lay a vinyl bag on the bench beside the old man. The old man would go nowhere without it. Even at a glance, it resembled its owner very much, worn-out, rumpled, and hollow. Thrown as it might be into a garbage can, no one would be tempted to pick it up. He looked up at the old man's face. Only then did he notice a cut on his father's forehead.

"Dear me! What's happened to your forehead?" he cried in surprise.

"Nothing, it's nothing," the old man said, waving his hand at him.

"Stay still for a second, please."

He moved up close to his father and looked into the cut. It looked like a scratch made by a stick or something. It stood out much more against the

「어데! 앵경은 그전에 뿌사진 기다.」

노인은, 마치 잘못을 저지른 아이처럼 낯빛을 붉혔다.
「저으게 나무 밑을 지나오다 보이꺼네 머가 이마에 턱
안 걸리나. 솔가지 하나가 축 처진 거를 보고 내 딴에는
피한닥고 피한 기 고마 이래된 기라. 요새 내 잘 당한대
이. 눈이 침침한 기 당최 짐작이 없다카이. 아무데나 허
연 대가리 잘 디받고 산다 마.」

단순한 시력감퇴만 아니라, 그만한 나이에 이르면 일
종의 공간감각 같은 게 둔해지기도 하는 모양이라고 그
는 생각하였다.

「우야겠노, 그기 다 늙은 탓 아이겠나. 걸어댕기는 일
도 전만은 몬 한 거 같더라. 이노무 발이 자꼬 헛디딜락
해서 자 타고 할 석마다 애묵는다카이. 살 자빠지기도
한대이. 옛말에, 그래서 늙으마 섧다 안카더나.」

노인은, 이번에는 소리를 내지 않고 웃는다. 그는 왠
지 맥이 탁 풀리고 말아서 아무런 대꾸도 못하였다. 문
득 하늘을 쳐다보았다. 관악산 위 하늘을 붉게 물들였
던 놀이 잿빛으로 식어 가고 있었다. 또 한 대의 비행기
가 산 너머로 미끄러져 내렸다.

「약이라도 좀 발라야지요?」

bald part of his head, receding from the forehead all the way to the crown. Slightly off the center of his forehead and to the right was a scratch, a straight line about two finger joints long, which made the old man look all the more miserable; he couldn't help being overcome by sudden waves of compassion for his aged father. Judging by the blood still drying in the scratch, it had probably happened only a few hours before. He then noticed the old man's broken glasses. Obviously, he had bumped his head hard against something.

"What on earth happened? You even got your glasses broken. It must've been a really big accident! Where'd it happen?"

Asking one question after another, he felt his own shoulders going limp. His spirits couldn't sink any further.

"No, that's not it! The glasses were already broken before the accident."

The old man blushed like a child who had done something wrong. "When I was walking under the tree over there, something suddenly brushed against my forehead. One of the pine branches was hanging low, so I thought to avoid it as quickly as I could, only to end up this way. These days, I get

한참 만에 그는 말하였다. 「그래야 빨리 아물지요.」

「개안타 마, 나도라!」

노인은 손사래를 쳤다. 「이까짓 거 가주고 남사시럽
거로 약은 무신 약이고! 나도라 고마.」

하긴 그렇기도 하다고, 그는 맥없이 고개를 주억거렸
다. 이마 한가운데라 빨간약을 바르기도 그렇고, 반창
고 같은 것을 붙여두기에는 더 요란스럽기만 하리라고
생각하였다. 이따 집에 들어가는 길로 연고 같은 거나
찾아봐야겠다고 그는 작정하였다.

「그 안경 좀 보십시다.」

한참 뒤에 그는 말하였다.

「앵경도 개안타카이.」

노인은 그러면서 안경을 벗어 건네주었다. 그는 잔잔
히 그것을 들여다보았다. 이 또한, 참 그럴 수 없다 싶게
주인을 쏙 빼어 닮은 물건이었다. 검정 뿔테안경으로
너무나 무겁고 투박한 구닥다리였다. 그 역시 줄잡아
30년 이상 안경을 써온 사람이지만, 그 같은 물건은 아
마도, 이제는 골동품 가게에나 가야 구경할 수 있으리
라고 짐작되었다. 그나마 다리 한쪽은 색깔이나 굵기가
생판 엉뚱하였다. 원래 제짝이 아닌 거다. 게다가 또, 불

into accidents like this quite often. My eyes have gotten so dim, I can't quite make out things around me. I'm going around butting my white head into this and that all over the place."

It seemed more than just the old man's failing eyes, though. Perhaps, at his father's age, one's sense of space also tends to become dull, he thought.

"What can I do about it? It's all because I'm old, isn't it? Walking around isn't what it used to be, either. These darn feet of mine keep losing their footing, giving me so much trouble whenever I get on the bus or something. I'm also falling over all the time. As the old saying goes, 'Woe are the aged.'"

The old man laughed, silently this time. Feeling drained of energy for some reason, he couldn't say anything in response. He looked up into the sky. The glow that had dyed the sky over Mt. Gwanak crimson was cooling into ashen dusk. Another airplane flew away over the mountain.

"Shouldn't you put some medicine on it?"

Then, after a good while, he added, "It'll help it heal quick."

"It'll be okay. Leave it be!"

51

에 태운 자국까지 나 있었다. 아마 당신이 손수 모양을 바로잡아보려고 연탄불 같은 데다 올려놓았다가 그 지경을 만든 게 분명하다고 그는 생각하였다.

「이거 맞춘 지 얼마나 됩니까?」

혀를 차고 싶은 마음으로 그는 물었다.

「하마 5, 6년은 됐을 꺼로?」

보기보다는 오래지 않다고 생각되었으므로 무심중에 그는 말하였다.

「그런데 어째 이래 험하지요? 제 것도 그 정도 썼지만 아직 이처럼 말짱한데요?」

「테는 원래 쓰던 거 아이가. 알만 새거고 테는 중고품으로 안 했나. 씰데없이 테 값을 너무 달락 해서…… 그래노 끄떡없이 잘만 뵈더라.」

그는 깨진 알을 다시 꼼꼼히 들여다보았다. 졸보기와는 반대로 가운데가 볼록한 게 꽤나 무게가 느껴졌다. 엉뚱하게도 그 중량감이 기억 한 가닥을 떠올리게 하였다. 그랬다. 그 무렵에 당신은 눈수술을 하셨지. 한동안 눈이 침침해지더니 끝내는 앞이 보이지 않는다고 했었다. 노인네들에게 흔히 있는 백내장이었다. 수술은 그다지 까다로운 게 아니었다. 당신 경우에는 혈압이 다

The old man waved his hand. "Don't fuss over nothing, it's embarrassing. Forget the medicine!"

The old man made sense. He nodded his head weakly. It wouldn't do to put the red Mercurochrome right in the middle of his forehead. A Band-Aid would be overdoing it. He thought he would look for an ointment of some sort as soon as he got into his apartment.

"May I take a look at your glasses?" he asked after a while.

"Nothing's wrong with the glasses, either."

His father said, handing over the glasses. He took time examining them. Incredibly, the glasses were the spitting of their owner, too. The black horn-rimmed spectacles were much too heavy and crude and were well out of date. He himself had been wearing glasses for at least thirty years, but he knew that glasses of the kind were no longer seen outside antique shops. Further, one of the legs was outrageously different from the other and the rest of the frame in both color and thickness. It wasn't the original leg. Worst of all, there was a burn mark on the frame. Apparently, his father had put it on something like a briquette fire to fix its crookedness himself.

소 장애요소가 되긴 하지만 그것도 우려할 정도는 아니라는 게 담당 의사의 소견이었다. 과연 수술은 성공적이었고, 뒤도 깨끗하였다. 당신은 다시 평소의 시력—시원치는 못하나 그럭저럭 견딜 만은 한—을 되찾았던 것이다. 그러나, 만사가 잘 끝났다고는 해도, 수술 중에나 그 직후에나 얼굴 한번 디밀지 못하고 지나버린 일이 그로서는 오랫동안 마음에 걸렸었다. 그런데 바로 그 기막힌 안경이 그때 맞춘 것이라는 얘기였다. 수술비에 충당하십사고 약간 액을 온라인 구좌로 송금했을 뿐, 이런저런 사정을 스스로 핑계하고 끝내 가보지 못하였던 부끄러움이, 이제 그 만신창이 구닥다리 안경으로 하여 새삼스레 목덜미를 붉게 만들었다.

그는 손수건을 꺼내어 안경알을 정성껏 닦았다. 당신은 한 달이 가도 제대로 한 번 닦아 쓰는 법이 없는 듯 먼지로 절어 있었다. 렌즈와 테가 맞물린 부분에는 기름때가 끈끈하게 달라붙어 있어서 수건 따위로 닦아내기란 아예 불가능하였다. 간신히 렌즈의 가운데 부분만 공들여 닦은 다음, 그는 제 것을 벗고 대신 써보았다. 아무것도 분별할 수가 없었다. 사물의 상들이 온통 뿌옇게 뭉개지고, 이상한 꼴로 뒤틀리고, 몽롱하게 멀어져

"When did you get them?" He felt like clucking his tongue at him.

"It's already been five or six years, I guess."

They weren't as old as he had thought, so he blurted out:

"Why does the frame look so beaten then? Mine's as old as yours, but it still looks as good as new, doesn't it?"

"I got the frame secondhand in the first place, you see. Lenses were new, but the frame was secondhand. A new one cost way too much, it was ridiculous! I've had absolutely no problem seeing things, even with the used frame."

He inspected the broken lens meticulously once more. Unlike the lens for near-sightedness, it was bulgy in the center and heavy. The heftiness jogged in his mind a strand of a long-forgotten memory: A few years before his father had had an eye operation. For some time before the operation, his father complained about dimness in his eyes, which eventually led to a complete loss of sight. It turned out to be glaucoma, a common disease among elderly people. The operation itself was not a difficult procedure. His father's blood pressure could pose a bit of an obstacle, but according to

보였다. 그는 얼른 안경을 벗었다. 어쩌면 그 탁하고 왜곡된 풍경이야말로 항시 당신을 둘러싸고 있는 일상적 세계의 진면목인지도 모른다는 생각이 들자 가슴이 먹먹하고 답답해졌다. 그는 안경을 그 주인에게 되돌려주었다.

그리고는 맥 빠진 소리로 중얼댔다.

「자주 닦아 쓰세요. 먼지나 때가 젤로 잘 타는 물건이 이겁니다. 이거 쓰시고도 잘 보인다니 아버지는 참 무던두 하십니다.」

노인이 소리 내어 웃었다.「내사 개안타. 시상 돌아가는 일 머 할라꼬 눈에 불 키고 디리다볼 끼고. 마 대강대강 보고 사는 기지…… 내사 하낫도 안 불편타.」

「예, 그 말씀도 맞네요.」그도 웃어버리고 밀었다.

「그렇기는 해도 이 안경은 너무하네요. 오신 김에 짬 봐서 새 걸로 바꾸십시다.」

「어데, 내는 개안타카이!」

노인이 마구 손사래를 쳤다.「내가 살마 얼매나 더 살겠노. 이런 데다 백죄 돈 들일 꺼 없다. 내사 이거 기냥 쓸란다. 당최 돈 쓸 생각 마래이.」

「그래도 남 보기 답답해요.」

the doctor in charge, it shouldn't be too big of a problem. Indeed, the operation was successful with no complications afterwards. His father had his eyesight back, which was not that great, but tolerable. All ended well at the time, but the fact that he never went to see his father during, or even after the operation weighed heavily upon his conscience for a long time.

Now, the fact of the matter was that his father had gotten these ridiculous-looking spectacles around that time after the operation. He remembered wiring a small amount of money into his father's online bank account to cover the charges for the operation; but then he never managed to visit his father, always making this or that excuse to himself. Now, the beaten, antiquated spectacles triggered a fresh onslaught of shame, making him blush down to his neck.

He took out his handkerchief and wiped the lenses carefully. The thick dust covering the lenses indicated his father had failed to clean them properly even once a month. The sticky grime stuck in the grooves between the lenses and the rims were impossible to wipe off with a thing like a handkerchief. He barely managed to clean the middle parts

「삘시럽은 데 신경 쓴다. 차말이라 안 카나. 내가 개안 타카는데 너 거가 와 그캐쌓노?」

「예예, 알았습니다.」 그는 손을 들고 만다. 「그럼 아버지 편한 대로 하세요. 언제 저희들 말 따르셨습니까.」

그의 대꾸가 좀 퉁명스럽게 들렸던 모양이다. 노인은 갑자기 입을 다물고 시선을 내리깔았다. 그러고는 땅바닥을 무연히 내려다보며 소리 없이 어설픈 웃음을 짓고 있었다. 왠지 노인의 귓불이 한순간 붉어지는 듯싶었다. 마른 잡초처럼 귀 언저리에 초라하게 남아 있는 머리카락들이 그의 눈에 알알하게 와 박혔다.

며칠 전 일이었다. 그가 4교시 수업을 막 끝내고 나와 보니 동료 선생 여러 명이 교무실 앞 복도에 웅성거리고 서 있었다.

「뭣들 하자는 짓거리여?」

예사스럽게 그는 농을 던졌다. 마침 점심시간을 앞둔 때였다. 보나마나, 작당하여 밖으로 나가자는 수작이라고 그는 생각했던 것이다.

「손금 보러 가자는 야그지 시방?」

손금보기란 두말할 것도 없이 섰다를 가리킨다. 특별

of the lenses carefully; and after taking off his own glasses, he tried them on. He couldn't make out anything around him. All the objects blurred out of their shapes beyond recognition, looking twisted and hazily distant. He quickly removed them. When it occurred to him that the muddy and distorted sights could be the realities of the everyday world surrounding his father, he felt stunned and frustrated. He returned the spectacles to their owner. Then he murmured in a tired voice:

"You should clean these more often. Glasses get dirty and grimy easily. You're saying you can see well with these? You must be an extremely patient person."

The old man laughed aloud. "I'm okay with these. What's the good of looking into worldly affairs? All I want is just the rough ideas, that's all. Nothing's wrong with my glasses."

"Yes, I take your point too," he also laughed it off.

"Having said that, these glasses are beyond salvaging, Father. Now you're here, let's get you a new pair."

"What are you talking about? I said the old pair's all right with me!"

The old man waved his hand very hard. "How

한 건수가 없는 한, 그들은 으레 그런 식으로 밥값을 해결해왔던 것이다. 그 방법의 장점은, 이유 없이 어느 한 사람에게 부담을 지우지 않으면서도, 그렇다고 더치페이라고 하는 저 삭막한 새 풍속을 연출하지 않아도 된다는 데 있었다. 주문한 음식이 나오기까지의 불과 10, 20분 동안에 지나지 않지만, 왁자지껄한 웃음과 승부수에 따른 긴장감 따위는 가외의 덤이랄 수 있었다.

그런데, 어쩐지 저쪽의 반응이 수상쩍었다. 전에 없이 어정쩡한 태도들이던 것이다. 그들은 한동안 서로의 얼굴만 멀뚱멀뚱 쳐다보며 우물쭈물하고들 있더니 마침내 그중 한 사람이 불쑥 말한다는 게 이런 식이었다.

「어이, 서형. 시골집에 전화 한번 넣어보지 그래?」

「무슨 뜬금없는 소리여 그게?」

그는 뜨악하게 물었다. 「시골집이라니? 서울집이 아니고?」

「당신 본가 말이야, 대구!」

「근 왜?」

「아, 문안전화 같은 거 할 수 있는 거잖어? 당신 말이야, 아버님과 통화한 지도 오래되지 아마? 사람이 그러면 못쓴다고. 그것두 훈장질하는 위인이 말야. 애들 보

much longer will I live? No need to spend money at all on things like this. I'll keep wearing them. Don't you dare think of wasting money."

"But you're embarrassing others by wearing them."

"Don't worry yourself about it. I keep telling you the truth. I'm alright already!"

"Yes, yes, I've got it." He finally gave up. "Please, do as you wish, Father. You've never followed our advice anyway, have you?"

Perhaps, the old man sensed some curtness in his response. He suddenly fell silent, casting his eyes down. But as he stared down at the ground dejectedly, he forced an awkward smile. For some reason, the old man's earlobes seemed to turn red for a moment. The sad, disheveled hair that remained sparsely around his ears, looking like dried weeds, burned into the son's eyes.

It was a few days earlier. When he came back to the staff room right after the 4th period ended, several of his fellow teachers were in the corridor outside the room, talking about something among themselves.

"What are you people up to?" He cracked non-

기 부끄럽지두 않어? 그러니까 지금이락두 후딱 문안 인사 드리라구, 어서!」

그는 그제야 가슴이 싸늘하게 얼어붙는 충격을 받았다. 머릿속이 갑자기 텅 비어 버려서 그는 한참을 우두망찰 서 있기만 하였다. 누군가가 등을 떼밀었다. 비로소 그는 황망히 전화기 앞으로 달려갔고, 그리고 장거리 전화를 시도하였다. 지역번호를 돌리고, 국번을 돌리고, 그리고…… 당황한 나머지 마지막 네 자리가 기억나지 않았다. 그는 송수화기를 팽개치고 나서 호주머니 여기저기를 뒤져 수첩을 꺼내들었다. 누군가가 다가와 주의를 주었다. 그 순간, 신통하게도 네 자리 숫자가 나란히 떠올랐다. 그는, 수첩을 팽개치고 나서 다시 전화통에 달라붙었다. 옆에서 누군가가 또 말하였다. 천천히 하라구. 그래, 천천히……

그때 신호음이 끊어지면서 누군가의 기척이 저쪽에서 나왔다.

「대구지요?」

댓바람에 그는 소리쳤다.「거기, 고성동 아닙니까?」

못지않게 긴장되고 어눌진 목소리가 저쪽에서 대꾸하고 있었다.「예, 대구 맞심더. 고성동 맞으예. 누구 찾

chalantly.

As it happened, it was just before the lunch time. He just thought they were, as usual, cooking up an excuse to go somewhere outside the school.

"You're gonna get your palms read, right?"

Getting palms read meant playing the Sotta card game, of course. Unless it was a special occasion, they had always taken care of their meal expenses that way. It had the advantage of not having to burden one person with the lunch bill for the entire group with no reason, while avoiding the new, heartless custom called Dutch treat. The game lasted only ten to twenty minutes before their orders came out, but their robust laughter and the tense anticipation of the winning move and so forth were a welcome throw-in.

That day, however, he felt something odd in the others' behavior. They seemed awkward and hesitant for some reason, which was quite unusual. For a while, they looked at one another silently until one of them blurted out:

"Hey, brother Seo, why don't you try calling home in the country?"

"What on earth are you talking about?"

Confused, he asked, "Home in the country? You

심니꺼?」

대답에 앞서 그는 잠긴 한숨부터 후루룩 토해냈다. 약간 쉬고, 낮고, 떨리는 듯한 목소리—그것은 의심의 여지없이 아버지의 음성이 분명하였던 것이다. 그는 악을 쓰듯이 마구 외쳐댔다.

「아부지, 접니다. 학굽니다. 예, 별고 없으시고요? 건강은요? 예, 예, 다들 별일 없으시지요?」

저쪽에서 되돌아오는 말인즉슨 언제나 다를 것이 없었다. 별고 없다, 무슨 일이 있겠느냐, 건강도 좋다, 모다 탈 없이 잘 있으니 걱정할 것 없다—말하자면 그런 식이었다. 그러고 나서 내처 이쪽의 안부를 되물어왔다.

「너거는 어떠노? 앗들은 핵교 잘 댕기고? 니는? 요새도 왔다 갔다 하나? 욕본다. 너거 안사람도 건강하제?」

이번에는 그가 한차례, 익숙하게 답변하였다. 이쪽도 무사하며, 애들도 학교 잘 다니고 있고, 자신은 물론 변함없이 원거리 통근 중이며, 집사람도 건강에 이상 없다—대충 그런 사연들을 줄줄이 늘어놓는 식이었다.

어떻게 보면 매번 숨이 차는 느낌이었다. 쫓기듯이 한바탕 의례적인 말들을 주고받고 나면 대화는 금세 바닥이 나버렸다. 더 이상 해야 할 말이 남아 있지 않는 것이

don't mean my home in Seoul?"

"Your parents' in Daegu!"

"Daegu? Why?"

"Well, you can just give them a call to inquire after their health or something, can't you? You probably haven't talked to your father for a long time, have you? You should know better, and as a teacher too. Aren't you ashamed to face the kids? So, hurry up and give your father a call, now!"

Only then did he feel a heart-freezing shock. He couldn't think of anything as if his brain were hollowed out. He just stood there dumbfounded for a long while. Someone nudged him from behind. Then he rushed to the telephone and tried to make a long-distance call. Area number, exchange number, and...? He, in such a flurry, couldn't remember the last four digits. He dropped the handset and rummaged through his pockets to finally produce a small notebook. Somebody came over to him and told him to calm down. At the moment, miraculously, all four digits, in the right order, came to him. He dropped the notebook and turned back to the telephone. Someone beside him told him again, "Take it easy. Yes, that's it. Don't rush..."

Just then, the ringing stopped and someone was

었다. 장거리 전화를 통해 매번 확인하게 되는 것은, 부자간에도 별로 나눌 만한 얘기가 없다는 사실이었다. 서로 떨어져 산다는 것, 그래서 도무지 살을 비벼댈 기회가 없다는 것—그것의 삭막한 의미를 새삼 확인받는 느낌이곤 하였다.

이럴 때 항용 서둘러 통화를 끝내는 쪽은 아버지였다. 이번 역시 예외가 아니었다. 문안인사가 한차례 오가고 나자 곧「다른 용건이 있능 거는 아이제?」하고 저쪽에서 물어왔고, 그렇다고 그가 답변하기가 무섭게「그라마 전화 끊자, 백죄 요금 올릴 거 있나. 고마 들어가거라.」그리고는, 이쪽에서 뭐라 더 말을 붙일 쯤도 없이 통화는 끊어지고 말았다.

그는 무너지듯 풀썩 주저앉았다. 전신의 맥이 쇠 풀려 버린 것 같았다. 송수화기를 잡았던 자리가 땀에 젖어 번들거렸다. 목 뒷골이 쾅쾅 패고 빳빳해지는 느낌이었다. 간신히 고개를 쳐들자 동료들이 헐겁게들 웃고 있었다.

「뭐 하자는 짓들이야 이거?」

그는 냅다 고함을 질렀다.「누구 졸도하는 꼴 보구 싶은 거야?」

there at the other end.

"Did I get Daegu?"

He immediately yelled into the phone. "Isn't it Goseong-dong?"

A voice, which was as tense and inarticulate as his own, answered at the other end.

"Yes, this is Daegu, Goseong-dong. Who are you calling?"

Before answering, he breathed out a long-held sigh. There was a slightly hoarse, low, trembling voice—it was without a doubt his father's. He talked loudly, almost at the top of his lungs.

"Father, it's me. From school. Yes. How are you? How about your health? Yes. Yes. Are you all doing well?"

His father's replies were the same as usual: "No problem. What on earth could have happened? I'm in good health. Everyone else is doing well too, so there's nothing to worry about." Then his father began to inquire after his family.

"What about your family? Are the kids doing okay at school? And you? Are you still traveling back and forth? Must be hard on you. Is your wife in good health, too?"

And then, it was his turn to go through the famil-

「아, 미안 미안! 진정하라구.」

그들의 해명인즉 이러하였다.「좀 전에, 당신 나오기 한 30분 전에 말이야, 요상한 전활 받았었다구. 저기, 총무과 김양이 말이야. 누군가 당신을 찾으면서, 부친상을 입었으니 빨리 오라고 하더라는 거야. 김양이 얼굴이 하얗게 돼 가지고 와서 그러잖아 글쎄. 아, 그러니 우리도 당연히 긴장할 수밖에. 안 그래?」

「그래서?」

그는 다잡아 물었다.「대구서 왔대?」

「한데 말이야, 바로 고 대목이 좀 모호하더라구. 대구가 아니라 엉뚱하게 순천 어디라나? 그래서 전활 해보란 거지. 김양이 잘못 들었을 수도 있잖아? 쇼크 먹구서 말이야.」

남들은 피식피식 웃고들 있었지만 그로서는 그럴 만한 기력이 도무지 남아 있지 않았다. 이상하게도 몹시 짙은 피로감 속에 빠져들었다. 시들하게 그는 묻고 있었다.

「그럼 어떻게 되는 얘기야?」

「어디선가 초상이 난 건 확실해. 장난일 수야 없지. 누군가가 정말 부친상을 당한 거라구.」

iar series of replies: His family was all well. Kids were happy at school. He still continued the long-distance commuting. Nothing was wrong with his wife's health.

In a way, it always made him gasp for breath. After the exchange of ceremonial words, rushed as if they were chasing after them, they quickly ran out of subjects to talk about. There was nothing left to say. Through the long-distance conversations, he always felt convinced that there was really nothing much to talk about even between father and son. He felt as though he was reminded again and again of the dreary consequences of family members living apart with no chance to become part of each other's everyday life.

At times like these, it was usually his father who hastily ended the phone conversation. That day was no exception. As soon as they finished exchanging greetings, his father asked, "There isn't anything else you want to talk about, is there?" When he said no, his father immediately responded: "Okay then, let's say good-bye for now. Why raise the rates on the phone bill? I'll let you go now." And he hung up before he even had a chance to say anything.

그는 또 물었다. 「그럼 그게 누구야?」

「글쎄, 우선 서형하고 이름자가 비슷한 사람이겠지. 직업도 그렇고, 근무지도…… 단지 고향만 다른 거야. 가까운 이웃동네서 근무하고 있는 사내일는지도 몰라. 어때, 그렇지 않을까?」

그럴듯한 추리야. 그거, 말 되네, 말이 된다구. 다들 머리를 주억거리면서 밖으로 몰려나갔다. 그날만은 손금 보기를 하지 않았다. 이런 유의 일을 당할수록 당사자의 명은 더 길어진다는, 도무지 근거는 없으나 그렇다고 기분 나쁠 것까지는 없는 주장을 펴면서 동료들이 한턱을 은근히 강요했으므로 그가 쾌히 밥값을 떠안았던 것이다.

엉뚱한 선화 때문에 _노_가 받은 충격은 그러나 그것으로 끝나지 않았다. 그는 그날 밤에도 또 한 번 상을 당하는 소동을 치렀던 것이다. 이번에는 꿈속에서의 일이었다. 아버지의 시신 앞에서 얼마나 격렬하게 통곡했던지 옆방의 하숙 동료가 그를 깨우러 건너왔을 정도였다.

「무슨 꿈이게 그래?」 동료가 하품을 하며 물었다.

「친상 당하는 꿈이야.」 뗩뜰하게 그는 대꾸하였다.

「아따 그 양반, 참 오래 사실랑가보요.」

He flopped down helplessly on the floor. His whole body seemed to be completely drained of energy. The palm of his hand that held the handset glistened with sweat. The back of his neck was stiff and throbbing. When he barely raised his head, his colleagues were smiling sheepishly.

"What on earth are you trying to do to me?" He yelled at them, "Do you want to see me faint?"

"Ah, we're so sorry, so sorry. Calm down now."

They explained: "About half an hour before you left class, we had a strange phone call. You know Miss Kim over in the General Affairs Department, right? She said someone asked for you and said your father had passed away, so you needed to come home right away. She came to us with the news, so pale in the face. Well, think about it. We couldn't help getting all tensed up, could we?"

"So?"

He urged them. "Was it from Daegu?"

"That's the thing, you see. That part was a bit amiss. It wasn't Daegu, but Suncheon or someplace else. So, that's why we asked you to call your father. Miss Kim could have heard it wrong, couldn't she have? Since she was in such a terrible shock."

They were all smiling shyly, but he had no ener-

71

자못 성가시다는 듯이, 동료는 투덜대며 건너가버렸다. 곧 코 고는 소리가 들려왔다. 하지만 그는 오래 잠을 이루지 못하였다. 저 꿈속의 울음 한 자락이 여전히 목구멍에 남아 있는 것 같았다. 몸을 이리 뒤척 저리 뒤척하면서 그는 새삼스레 낮의 일을 되새김질하였다.

연전에 고희를 넘겼으니 올해 일흔둘이다. 평균 수명이 길어졌다고는 해도, 그 연세면 결코 적은 것이 아니라고 그는 생각하였다. 비교적 건강한 편이기는 해도, 노인의 건강은 아무도 자신할 수 없는 법, 언제 화급한 일을 당하게 될지 도무지 예측할 수 없다는 사실 앞에서 그는 새삼 두려움을 느꼈다. 창졸지간에 상을 당한다─그러면 어떻게 되나? 그는 두려움에 짓눌린 채로 골똘히 생각에 잠겼다.

제일 먼저 떠오른 것은 장례 문제였다. 당연히 자신이 떠맡아야 할, 맏상주로서의 역할이 마음을 무겁게 하였다. 무엇 하나 준비돼 있는 것이 없다고 생각되었다. 정작 어느 쪽에서 치러야 할지도 막연한 노릇이었다. 대구 바닥은, 그로서는 객지와 다름없는 곳이었다. 어린 나이에 그곳을 떠났기 때문이었다. 50, 60년대의 대구를 회상하면 그의 마음의 눈에는 언제나 역전 공회당

gy left in him to do the same. Strangely, he felt himself falling into a thick fog of fatigue. He found himself asking reluctantly.

"What does all that mean, then?"

"One thing is certain. Someone's passed away. It couldn't have been a prank. Someone's father has passed away."

He asked again. "Who is it then?"

"Well, first of all, he must be someone with a name similar to yours. And then, the same job, the same workplace... The only difference is the hometown. It could be a man working in our neighborhood. What do you think? Doesn't that make sense?"

"That's sound reasoning. That makes sense, it really does." Nodding their heads, they all filed out of the room. That day, they didn't read palms. Instead, he ended up treating them, gladly though, encouraged by their claim that each time a person gets mistaken for a dead person, his life would end up much longer, which was completely groundless and yet not at all unpleasant to hear.

However, the impact of the odd episode on him lingered on even after the lunch. That night, he experienced the death of his father once more. This

건물 벽에 내걸린 군인극장 간판이 보이고, 밤낮없이 장사치들이 아글바글하던 양키시장 골목과 자갈마당, 그리고 어느 해던가 야당 선거 유세장이던 수성천변의 똥구덩이들 따위가 선하게 떠오르곤 하였다. 하지만 오늘의 대구직할시에 그런 모습은 이미 남아 있지 않다. 그것처럼 대구는 이제 그에게는 낯선 도시 중 하나일 뿐이었다. 물론 일가붙이들이 전혀 없는 것은 아니었다. 더러 있다고는 해도 낯설기는 마찬가지였다. 언제 상면할 기회가 있었던가. 피차 얼굴을 잊고 산 지가 기억조차 아득한 처지였다.

그렇다고 해서 상주 편하자고 서울 쪽을 일방적으로 고집할 일도 못 된다고 그는 또 생각하였다. 서울 쪽이라고 사정이 나을 것 역시 없는 까닭에서였다. 무엇보다, 서민 아파트라고 하는, 옹색한 공간이 당장 문제였다. 사람 사는 마을이라면 당연히 송장 치는 일도 있게 마련이어서 평소 듣기도 하고 더러 보기도 하지만, 어쨌거나 그런 일에 아파트처럼 불편하고 민망스러운 환경은 달리 없다고 생각되었다. 사실인즉 평수의 문제가 이미 아닌 것이었다. 그것 한 가지만으로도, 흔히 말하는 아파트 생활의 편리함을 깡그리 상쇄시킬 만하다고

time, it was in his dream. He cried so much in front of his father's body in the dream that his fellow boarder, living in the room next to his, came over to wake him.

"What was the dream about?" his next-room neighbor asked, yawning.

"My father's passed away in the dream." He answered gloomily.

"Good lord! Is he ever gonna live a long life!"

The neighbor went away grumbling, bothered for nothing. Soon, he heard the neighbor snoring. However, he couldn't fall asleep for a long time. A trace of his wailing in the dream seemed to stay on in his throat. Tossing and turning, he thought long and hard over what had happened earlier that day.

His father had had his 70th birthday a couple of years before, so he was now 72. Though the average span of life had become longer, he thought, his father's age was still not something one should consider "still okay." His father was relatively healthy, but he knew the health of an elderly person could never be guaranteed. Confronted with the fact that he could never foresee when the inevitable would happen to him, he suffered a heightened sense of fear. 'What am I supposed to

그는 늘 생각해오던 터였다. 그런 점에서라면 비록 간신히 바라크를 면할 정도의 초라한 집이기는 할지언정 대구 쪽이 한결 나으리라는 생각이 들었다.

그것만도 아니다. 장례의식도 문제가 되었다. 아내의 강권 탓이라고는 해도, 어쨌든 그는 명색이 기독교인이었다. 하지만 아버지는 물론, 다른 형제들도 종교와는 무관한 사람들이다. 따라서, 재래의 전통적 의식을 당연히 선호할 게 분명하였다. 어쩌면 이 문제를 둘러싸고 한바탕 분란이 빚어질는지도 모를 일이었다. 개인적으로는, 신앙과는 상관없이, 전통의례만은 피하고 싶었다, 그것은 상상만 해도 지겹고 구차스럽게 느껴졌다. 상복에서부터 제상에 이르기까지, 초혼에서부터 삼우제에 이르기까지 소도구 한 점, 절차 한 매듭 지긋지긋하지 않은 대목이 없었다. 그렇다고 기독교식이 썩 좋게 생각되느냐 하면 그도 아니었다. 그쪽도 마음에 내키지 않기는 매한가지였다. 아직 치러본 적이 없긴 하지만, 아마도 어딘가 좀 싱겁고 맹숭맹숭하지 않을까 싶은 것이다. 하지만 거기엔 참으로 중요한 미덕이 한 가지 있다고 그는 생각한다. 문장에 비유한다면, 전통적인 장의 절차가 만연체라고 할 때 기독교식은 간결체

do, then?' he was absorbed in this thought, over-whelmed by fear.

The first thing that came to his mind was the matter of funeral arrangements. As the oldest son, it was naturally his responsibility. He thought he hadn't gotten anything ready. To begin with, he had absolutely no idea where the funeral would be held. Since he left Daegu when he was very young, the city was now as unfamiliar as any other places that were foreign to him. Reminiscing about Daegu from the 1950s and 1960s, he always imagined the Soldiers Movies Theater sign on the wall of the town-hall building in front of the train station, the Yankee Market alleys crowded day and night with dealers, the Gravel Square, and the dung pits along the bank of the Susong River, which had been the opposition party's election campaign ground one year. However, in the now central-government-controlled Daegu City, no traces of the past could be found. That was exactly how he felt about Dae-gu, a city completely unfamiliar to him now. Of course, it wouldn't be true to say he had no family, other than his father, living there. Nevertheless, the city was foreign to him all the same. When had he ever had a chance to see them? He couldn't even

에 해당한다는 사실이 그것이었다. 그리고 그 점만으로도 그에게는 대단한 매력이 되었다. 아무려면 어떤가, 어느 쪽이든 무방하다—라고 대범하게 치부했다가도, 그게 또 결코 단순한 문제가 아닌 듯싶어 그는 생각을 자꾸만 되작이곤 하였다.

그러나 이날 밤 그의 마음을 무겁게 만든 것은, 다른 무엇보다 불효의 감정이었다. 장남이면서도 아버지를 끝내 모셔보지 못한 채 사별하고 말았다는, 그 돌이킬 수 없는 불효의 감정이 강렬하게 그를 사로잡았던 것이다. 낮에 있었던 저 전화 소동의 충격이나 꿈속에서의 그 격렬한 울음도 바로 거기에다 뿌리를 두고 있었다는 사실을 그는 비로소 깨달을 수 있었다.

정말 이러나가 어느 날 느닷없이 상을 낭하는 건 아닐까? 생각하기조차 두렵고 난감한 노릇이지만, 그러나 또 실상인즉 그럴 공산이 더 크다는 예감 앞에서 그는 정말 오랜 시간 잠을 이루지 못하였다.

갑자기 놀이터가 시끌덤벙해졌다. 아이들 한 떼거리가 몰려든 것이다. 계집애들이 재빨리 그네를 차지해버리자 사내아이들은 미끄럼틀 쪽으로 우르르 밀려갔다.

remember when was the last time he had ever gotten together with any one of them.

Nonetheless, he knew better than to insist on Seoul just for his, that is, the chief mourner's convenience. Even if he chose Seoul, things wouldn't be any better. Above all, the cramped space in his low-income-family apartment would be the immediate problem. In any village or town inhabited by people, one was bound to see or hear how the dead bodies were being removed. But he knew that nothing was more inconvenient and embarrassing than an apartment, regardless of its square footage, that was also a setting for a funeral. That particular inconvenience alone, he always believed, would cancel out all the so-called "conveniences of the apartment housing." In that sense, Daegu was a much wiser choice if the humble house over there was hardly any better than barracks.

In addition to the funeral site, there were other things to consider, for example, the funeral ceremony. Although he was primarily motivated by his wife, he had become and was known as a Christian now. However, his father and all of his brothers and sisters were not religious at all. Therefore, beyond all question they would all prefer the tradi-

지금까지 혼자서 그네에 매달려 있던 꼬마가 여자애들에게 슬며시 자리를 내주고는 그 옆의 시소로 옮겨 앉았다. 그리고는, 약간 겁먹은 것 같은 눈으로 주위를 두리번거렸다. 그 표정 하며 인상이 조금은 낯익은 기분이어서 그는 은연중에 미소를 띠었다. 노인도 그 모양을 지켜보고 있었던 모양이다. 불쑥 웃음을 터뜨리며 말하였다.

「니, 저 아 좀 보래이. 머스마가 우예 저렇기 숫기가 없을꼬? 맴 여린 거 하고, 꼭 니 어릴 때 겉다카이!」

「제가 말입니까?」 그도 소리 내어 웃었다.

「하모. 영판 저랬다 아이가. 동네 앗들한테 치이가주고 삽짝 밖을 잘 안 나갈라캤디라. 죽은 니 할매가 마실 갈 때마둥 억지로 데불꼬 댕기고 그랬다카이. 소핵교 댕기면서부텀 쪼매씩 나아지던 거로.」

할머니와 어머니의 치맛자락만 맴돌면서 살았던 어린 시절을 그는 잠시 회상하였다. 하지만 또렷하게 잡혀 나오는 기억은 없었다. 여름 장마철이면 잡풀이 무성하게 돋아나던 안마당이 잠시 떠올랐다. 가을이면 그곳은 타작마당이 되어버렸다. 새벽부터 기세 좋게 돌아가곤 하던 탈곡기 소리를, 그는 어렴풋하게 환청으로

tional ceremony. It could start some trouble. Personally, regardless of his religion, he wanted to avoid the traditional ceremony. Just thinking about it, he felt weary and humiliated. From the costume to the sacrificial table, from the first to the third memorial service, from the props to the procedures, everything was wearisome. Not that he believed the Christian funeral ritual was much better. He was reluctant to choose it, too. He had never experienced it firsthand, but he wondered if it wasn't too flat and sober in some ways. Nonetheless, he noted that it had one important merit. To use the analogy of writing styles, the traditional funeral procedure would be the verbose style and the Christian one the concise. By that merit alone, the Christian ceremony was considered a very attractive option to him. At one moment, he would say to himself generously, "What difference will it make? It's okay either way." In the next moment, however, he would wonder if it was indeed such a simple matter, and backtrack on his earlier thoughts.

Among the thoughts that weighed upon him that night, most taxing was the self-reproach that he had been an unfilial son. He was in the grips of

들었다. 언제쯤이던가, 아침에 일어나 뒤란으로 돌아가 보면, 감꽃이 지천으로 떨어져 땅바닥을 하얗게 뒤덮고 있던 때가? 여름 한철, 높다란 대청마루에 누워서 마음이 흠씬 젖도록 귀 기울이곤 하던 소나기 소리, 매양 코끝에 알싸하게 감겨들던 흙냄새…… 일테면, 삽짝 밖을 벗어나지 않고도 결코 지겹지 않았던 세계다. 그러나 지금은, 문 밖에서 나는 좀 피곤하다, 짜증스럽다 하고, 그는 속으로 투덜댔다.

아내는 돌아왔을까? 잠긴 문에 비로소 생각이 미쳤다. 두 세계를 견고하게 차단하고 있는 저 철제의 문— 그 문 밖에서 서성거리고 있는 자신의 처지가 새삼 난감하였다. 아버지만 아니라면 온 길을 되돌아가버리고 싶어졌다. 그놈의 문을 따고 늘어간다고 해서 무슨 신통방통할 게 있을 것인가.

하지만 그는 일어섰다. 어쨌거나 다시 한번 확인해볼 일이었다. 그는 맥 풀린 걸음걸이로 공중전화 부스를 찾아갔다. 그리고는 별반 기대도 없이 집으로 전화를 걸었다. 따르릉 따르릉, 신호음이 울리기 시작하였다. 그러자 또 그놈의 엉뚱한 기대감이 울컥 가슴을 치받았다. 굳이 따지자면, 상당한 시간을 죽인 셈이기는 하였

guilt, thinking that if his father passed away, it would mean he irrevocably failed to perform his filial duty as the oldest son, since he would have never had his father live with him and his family until the last day of his father's life. He realized for the first time that his sense of guilt was at the root of both the terrible impact the telephone episode had had on him earlier that day and his nocturnal wailing that very night.

'What if one day my father's death catches me off my guard?' It was dreadful and unbearable even to think about it; but then, he also had a premonition that it was very likely to happen, which kept him awake for the longest time.

Suddenly, it became very noisy in the playground. Many children thronged there to play. After the girls quickly claimed the swings to themselves, the boys rushed to the slides. The boy who had been alone on one of the swings handed his swing over to the girls meekly and moved to the seesaw next to the swing set. The boy looked around a bit timidly. He found the boy's facial expression and features familiar, which made him smile unwittingly. The old man must have been

다. 그새 아내가 귀가했을 수도 있다, 아니, 거의 확실히 귀가했을 것이다, 하고 그는 성급하게 단정하는 마음이 되었다. 세 번, 네 번, 다섯 번…… 신호음만 계속 울리고 있었다.

공중전화 부스에서 나온 그는 깊은 곤혹감에 빠졌다. 그러나 그것도 잠시, 곧 방향을 잡아 휘적휘적 걷기 시작하였다. 어쩌면 집전화가 고장일지도 모른다는 생각이 문득 들었기 때문이었다. 과거에도 그런 경우가 없지 않았다. 그는 5층까지의 계단을 단숨에 올랐다. 그리고는 숨을 헐떡거리면서 한참을 서 있었다. 문은 잠긴 그대로였다. 손잡이에 걸어둔 가방 역시 변함이 없었다. 주인의 부재를, 그것은 분명하게 알려주고 있었다. 그럼에도 불구하고 그는 도어의 손잡이를 쥐고 가만히 비틀어보았다. 완강한 저항감이 손바닥에 또렷이 전해져왔다. 그는 얼른 손을 뺐다. 왠지 목덜미가 홧홧하게 달아올랐다. 자신의 우스꽝스런 꼬락서니를 누군가가 훔쳐보고 있는 것만 같아 그는 황망히 돌아섰다. 1층 현관까지 그는 뛰다시피 굴러내렸고, 그리고는 뒤도 돌아보지 않고 놀이터를 향해 잰 발걸음을 놓았다.

「집에 갔더나?」노인이 고개를 빼고 물었다.

watching the boy. He burst into laughter and said:

"Look at the kid over there. Such a shy child, a boy at that! He looks so tenderhearted, just like you in your childhood!"

"Me? Was I like that?" he laughed, too.

"Of course. Exactly like that boy. You were bullied by the village kids, and you didn't want to step out of the twig gate. Your late grandmother forced you to come with her whenever she went out to visit someone. You began to get better little by little after you entered grade school."

He tried to recall the days of his childhood when he didn't want to venture out of the safe vicinity of his grandmother and mother. Nevertheless, he couldn't remember any particular episodes, except some images and scenes: the courtyard, overgrown with weeds during the summer rainy season. The courtyard would turn into a threshing ground in the fall, with the energetic threshing machine running from daybreak on. Even now, he thought he'd heard the faint sound of the machine coming from somewhere. When was it? He would get up in the morning and walk around the house to the backyard to find the ground thickly carpeted with white persimmon flowers. The sound of the

「예.」

짧게 대답하고 그는 노인의 곁에 털썩 주저앉았다. 마주보이는 관악산 발치로 어스름이 고이고 있었다. 기다린다는 것도 참 막연한 짓이군, 하고 그는 중얼거렸다. 아내 쪽에서야 굳이 귀가시간에 신경 쓸 이유가 없다고 생각되었다. 두 아이 녀석은 으레 귀가가 늦다. 이른바 수도권의 분교에 적을 두고 있는 큰놈은 평소 빨라야 아홉 시 열 시다. 또 고3짜리 둘째는 보충수업에다 자율학습까지 있어 자정 가까운 시간에나 돌아오곤 하였다. 아내의 귀가시간을 간섭하는 것은 아무것도 없다. 그 점에 관한 한 그녀는 제왕처럼 자유롭다고 그는 생각하였다.

「열쇠가 하나밖에 없더나? 몇 개 더 맹글지 그랬노.」

노인의 핀잔이었다. 「열쇠 맹그는 데 가마 직석에서 똑같응 거 맹글어 준데이. 그느마들, 재주 참 희한하니라.」

「예, 한 개 더 만들어야겠네요.」

그는 고작 맥 풀린 웃음을 지어 보였다. 실인즉 열쇠를 두 개나 더 복제했었다. 그래서 식구들이 죄 하나씩 가지고 다닌다. 단지 자기만 예외인 것이다. 집을 찾는

summer shower he listened for, lying on the wooden floor of the main open-hall, until his heart was completely soaked in the sound. And the pungent smell of the soil constantly wending its way into his nose... It was, as it were, a world where he was never bored even without having to go out from the twig gate. "But now, I'm a bit tired, irritated, outside," he muttered to himself.

He wondered if his wife had come home yet. The locked door rushed back into his mind. That iron door separated the two worlds. Thinking about himself waiting outside that door, he felt helpless all over again. If it had not been for his father, he would have loved to go back to his school. Even if he had opened that door, he knew he would not likely find anything wonderful waiting for him inside.

Nevertheless, he got up. He thought he should check again anyway. He walked languidly back to the phone booth. And without much expectations at all, he called home. The phone began ringing. At that moment, he felt that unreasonable sense of hope fire through his heart once more. To justify the hope, he had already killed quite a long time. In the meantime, his wife may have been back. No!

일이 한 달에 고작 한 번이라고 해도 역시 열쇠는 지니고 있어야겠다고 그는 마음먹었다. 어떻게 보면 그것은 실제 사용 여부 이상의 상징적 의미를 지닌다는 생각이 들었다. 한줌씩이나 되는 열쇠 꾸러미를 허리춤에다 흔히 차고 다니는 사람들을 그는 비로소 이해할 수 있을 것 같았다. 그것처럼 완전한 소유의 징표가 어디 있으랴. 아내는 물론, 내 아이들까지 가지고 다니는 것을 나는 갖고 있지 못하다. 나의 가정이란 생각은 어쩌면 착각인지도 모른다. 그들의 가정이라고 해야 마땅하다. 그러고 보니 자신은 늘 잠긴 문 밖에서 서성거리고 있었다는 느낌이 들었다. 아버지의 집을 떠나온 이래 지금 이 후줄근한 나이에 이르도록 말이다…… 그 깨달음은 몹시 씁쓸한 것이었기 때문에 그는 한동안 말을 잃어버렸다.

놀이터의 아이들이 하나둘 흩어지고 있었다. 어스름이 사방에서 묻어오고 있었다. 머잖아 가등이 들어올 판이었다. 한 떼거리의 새들이 머리 위 하늘을 가로질러 공원 쪽으로 날아갔다. 그러고 나자 갑자기 주위가 적막해졌다. 텅 빈 놀이터를 앞에 하고 그들 두 부자—진작 칠십 고희를 넘어선 아버지와 그리고, 오십 지천

She almost certainly was back, he rashly conclud-
ed. Three, four, five times...the ringing continued.

Leaving the booth, he felt greatly bewildered.
However, it didn't last long; soon, he began trudg-
ing in the direction of his apartment. It suddenly
occurred to him that his home phone could have
been out of order. It wouldn't have been the first
time. He ran up the stairs to the fifth floor in one
breath. Then he stood there for a long while, panting. The door remained locked. The bag he'd hung
on the doorknob was still there. Clearly, there were
no occupants. And yet, he grabbed the doorknob
and turned it carefully. He felt a force of stubborn
resistance in his palm. He instantly withdrew his
hand. He felt hot in the neck for some reason.
Feeling as if someone was secretly watching the ridiculous sight of him, he whirled around. After almost hurtling down to the entry hall on the ground
floor, he trotted towards the playground, without a
glance back.

"You've been up there?" The old man asked,
craning his neck towards him.

"Yes, Father."

He gave a short answer and then flopped down
beside the old man. At the foot of Mt. Gwanak,

명을 코앞에 둔 아들—만 처량하게 남겨진 꼴이었다. 노인이 피워 문 담배연기가 허공으로 서서히 풀려나가는 것을 그는 무연한 눈길로 지켜보고 있었다. 그러자 무언가 좀 색다른 감정이 천천히 가슴에 고여 들었다. 어쩐지 마음 편하고 아늑한 느낌이었다. 아버지의 존재를 이처럼 가깝게 느껴본 적이 이전에도 있었던가? 그는 문득 자문해보는 마음이 되었다. 금세 한 가닥 기억이 눈부시게 떠올랐다.

그랬다. 아주 어렸을 적 추억이다. 어디서였던가? 아마도 마을 앞 그 개울이었을 것이다. 갯가엔 조그만 모래톱이 있고 또 둔덕에는 키 큰 미루나무들이 늘어서서 여름 한철 내내 시원한 그늘을 드리워주던 거기 말이다. 우리는 멱을 감고 있었다. 그래, 나는 아버지의 가슴에 안긴 채 겁에 잔뜩 질려 있었지. 아버지가 깊은 물속에다 나를 자꾸만 내려놓으려 했던 거다. 그럴수록 나는 한사코 당신 목에 매달리며 싫다고 앙탈했었지. 그러던 어느 순간, 그랬다, 나는 누군가의 비명을 들었고, 그리고 물속으로 사정없이 처박혔다. 아, 그 순간의 느낌이란! 그 아뜩한 절망감…… 나중에 안 일이지만, 필사적으로 바둥거리던 내 발길질에 당신이 그만 불두덩

dusk was gathering. "Waiting's such an uncertain thing, too," he muttered. On the part of his wife, it was not necessary to pay attention to when she returned home. Their two children always came home late. The older one, who was enrolled at a so-called branch campus in the metropolitan area, would be back home around nine or ten at the earliest. The younger one, a senior in high school, would stay at school until around midnight, completing the self-regulated study hours as well as the supplementary lessons. There was nothing that meddled with her regarding the time of her homecoming. In that respect, she was as free as an empress, he thought.

"Is there only one key? Why didn't you make several copies?"

The old man scolded him. "At the locksmith's, you can make copies on the spot, you know. Those fellows, their skills are incredible."

"Yes, I should get one more made."

All he could do was smile wearily. As a matter of fact, his family had already had two copies made. That meant one for each member. He was the only exception. He now realized he needed a key for himself even if he came home only once a month.

을 걷어채였던 거다, 후후⋯⋯

　그때를 생각하고 그는 혼자서 히죽히죽 웃었다. 물속에서 한차례 허우적거린 다음 그는 다시 아버지의 가슴에 안겼었다. 그리고는, 물 밖으로 나와서까지도 한동안 떨어지지 않으려고 했었다. 하지만 언제까지나 아버지의 가슴에 매달려 있을 수야 없는 노릇이어서 결국은 불안스레 땅바닥 위로 내려섰던 것이다. 그로부터 얼마나 많은 세월이 흘러갔는가? 그럼에도 불구하고 다시는, 아버지를 그만치 가깝게 느껴본 적이 없었다고 그는 생각하였다.

　그는 벤치에서 벌떡 일어났다. 이렇게 무작정 목을 늘이고 있을 일이 아니었다. 오히려 좋은 기회일 수도 있었다. 모처럼 두 부자만의 오붓한 시간을 허락받은 셈이다. 그러자 곧 희한한 아이디어가 떠올랐다.

「가십시다 아버지!」

　그는, 노인의 그 낡은 비닐백을 집어 들며 말하였다. 「좀 편안하게 쉴 수 있는 데로 가자구요.」

　어느새 그는 몇 발짝 앞서 휘적휘적 길을 열고 있었다.

　생각했던 대로 목욕탕은 한가하였다. 평일에는 늘 그

In a sense, a key has a symbolic meaning beyond the practical purpose, he thought. Only then was he able to understand those who often carried a handful of keys in the waist of their trousers. What else could be as perfect a symbol of possession as the keys? *Even my children, not to mention my wife, have their own keys, but I don't. Perhaps, I'm mistaken to think that I have my family. It's their family, to put it correctly.*

Come to think of it, he had always been standing around outside the locked door—from the time he left his father's house as a youngster until now, when he was already at *this saggy* age. It was such a bitter revelation that he couldn't speak for a while.

The kids were leaving the playground one after another. Dusk was settling around them in all directions. Soon, streetlights would come on. A flock of birds flew across the sky overhead towards the park. Then, the surroundings abruptly turned desolate. Only two of them were left behind feeling wretched—the father who had already past seventy, the age of *gohui* one rarely reached, to use the old expression, and the son who was almost fifty, the age of *jicheonmyeong* when one comes to understand the grand design of Heaven. He vacantly

랬던 것이다. 주말이나 공휴일 같은 때나 한바탕 붐비곤 하는 게 아파트 단지의 목욕탕 사정이다. 그는 속으로 쾌재를 올렸다. 우리 사회에서 가장 값싸게 시간을 죽일 수 있는 곳 중 하나가 목욕탕이라는 사실을 그는 진작부터 잘 알고 있었다. 그것은 또, 길바닥에다 버리는 시간이 많은 사람이라면 누구나 잘 터득하고 있는 지혜이기도 하였다. 한 달에 한 번꼴로 지방에 있는 직장과 서울 변두리에 있는 가정 사이를 기왕에만도 10년 가까운 세월을 줄기차게 오르내려야 했던 그였다. 오며 가며 어쩔 수 없이 버려지는 그 자투리 시간들을 그는 대체로 목욕탕에서 보내곤 했던 것이다. 그가 늘 드나드는 버스터미널이나 기차역 주변의 목욕탕들에 대해서는 속사정을 죄나 꿰고 있는 판이었다. 요즘 서울 쪽에서는 대형 목욕탕들이 늘어나고 있는 추세다. 그런 곳은 내부시설도 엄청난데, 그에 비해 사용료는 싼 편이었다. 비좁고 냄새 나는 구닥다리 대중탕의 그것보다 기천 원 정도 차이여서 적자 운영은 아닐까 싶어 괜시리 눈치 보이는 때도 없지 않는 것이다. 목욕 문화가 사치스럽고 난만해진다는 것은, 어쩌면 정신문화의 퇴영을 뜻하는 건지도 모른다고 그는 생각한다. 자신을 포

watched the smoke from his father's cigarette uncoil through the air. Meanwhile, a somewhat unusual emotion slowly filled his heart. It was making him feel rather relaxed and safe. *Have I ever felt my father's existence this up close before?* He asked himself. Immediately, a dazzlingly vivid strain of memory surfaced in his consciousness.

It was when I was very young. Where was I? Probably, I was in the stream in front of our village. The stream was banked with a narrow strip of sands, which led to a low hill where lines of tall willow trees stood, casting down cool shades all summer through. We were washing and playing in the water. My father held me in his arms, frightened to death. My father kept trying to put me down in the deep water. The harder he tried, the more tightly I wrapped my arms around his neck, kicking and thrashing whenever I touched the water. Then, at some moment, I heard someone scream and my father dumped me into the water. Ah, what I felt at the moment! That dizzying sense of despair... Only later was I told that in my desperate struggle, I happened to kick my father in the crotch. Hu-hu-hu...

Recollecting the scene, he grinned to himself. *After a bout of floundering in the water, my father scooped me back into his arms. Even outside the water, I wouldn't*

함하여, 그런 곳에서 마냥 세월을 죽이고 있는 사람들을 보노라면 불현듯 그런 느낌에 붙잡히기도 하는 것이었다.

어쨌거나 한 가지 유감인 것은, 노인네가 이른바 목욕 문화에 익숙지 못하다는 점이었다. 노인은, 그를 따라 어영부영 목욕탕까지 오기는 했지만 이제부터 낯선 사람들 틈바구니에서 옷을 벗고 어쩌고 할 일이 도무지 엄두가 나지 않는 모양이었다. 자꾸 주위만 뚤레뚤레 둘러보며 엉거주춤 서 있을 따름이었다. 노인네의 잔약한 콧등을 무겁게 짓누르고 있는 검정 뿔테안경이 더 뿌옇게 흐려 보였다. 그쪽을 짐짓 외면한 채 그는 천천히 옷을 벗었다.

노인을 향해 돌아서기 전에 맨 마지막으로 안경을 벗었다. 나안으로는 0콤마로 시작되는 시력이다. 그 사실이 아버지에 대한 면구스러움을 얼마쯤 덜어주었다. 이윽고 그는 돌아섰다. 노인이 마지못해 남방의 단추들을 벗기느라 애를 쓰고 있었다. 그 손놀림이 몹시도 아둔하였다.

「가만 계세요, 지가 해드리께.」그는 다가섰다.

그러자 노인이 뒤로 주춤주춤 물러서며 황망히 말하

let go of my father. However, it wasn't possible to hang onto his arms forever, so I got down onto the ground in the end, though uneasily. How many years had passed since then? Through all those years, he realized, he had never felt his father as close as he had at that moment of his childhood.

He jumped to his feet. There seemed to be not much point in waiting there indefinitely, craning their necks out for his wife. It could be a wonderful opportunity. It was as if the father and son were given a rare chance to spend time together all by themselves. Just then, he suddenly came up with a crazy idea.

"Let's go, Father!"

He said, picking up the old man's old vinyl bag. "Let's go to someplace where we can rest more comfortably, shall we?"

He was already leading the way a few steps ahead, walking in his usual sluggish way.

As expected, the public bath was not crowded. It was always like that on weekdays. The public bath in the apartment complex was crowded only on the weekends or official holidays. He yelled for joy silently. He had known that in the Korean society,

였다.「아이다, 개안타. 나도라.」

그는 웃음을 문 채 잠시 기다렸다. 노인의 손이 아까 보다 더 허둥거리는 것 같았다. 그나마 헐렁하게 끼워져 있는 단추들을 자꾸 더듬거리기만 할 뿐 별 진척이 없었다. 그는 다시 다가섰다.

「그거 보세요. 아버지도 인제 비서 하나 데리고 다녀야겠습니다.」

그는 말하고 나서 쓸쓸하게 웃었다.

「노인네들 비서라카마 우선에 짝대기 아이가. 난도 인자 짝대기 짚고 댕기야 되지 싶으다.」

그러면서 노인도 덩달아 웃었다.「걷능 거는 개안타마는 멋보담도 차 타고 내리능 기 힘든다카이. 그늠어 빠스가 더 그렇데이. 운전수는 퍼뜩 내리락고 빵빵 깝처쌓제, 무르팍은 떨리고 머리는 어지럽제, 아이고 내사 마 한분 타고 내릴라카마 등때기서 진땀이 다 난다 아이가.」

「될 수 있는 대로 버스 같은 거 타지 마세요. 노인들한테는 위험해요.」

「그라마 멀 타노?」

「택시 타야지요 뭐.」

one of the cheapest places to kill time at was the public bath. In fact, it was a wisdom well known to whoever spent a lot of time in the street. Once a month, he had been traveling back and forth already for ten long years between his place of work in the country and home in the outskirts of Seoul. He had been spending the odd hours, inevitably created here and there while traveling, mainly in the public bathhouse. So, he had gained an extensive and detailed knowledge about what was going on inside the bathhouses he frequented around the express bus terminals or train stations. Lately, in Seoul, large-scale bathhouses were on the rise. They all had quality interior setups, but their admission was relatively cheep. Their fee was only a few thousand *won* more than that of the cramped, smelly, outdated public baths; he sometimes felt uneasy using the new facilities, wondering if they weren't in the red at all. In his opinion, the trend of luxurious and splendid bathhouse culture could have been the reflection of retrogression in spiritual culture. Watching the people, including himself, doing nothing in there but kill time, he got caught up in such a train of thought.

Anyway, to his chagrin, the old man was not used

「뭐라카노? 돈도 돈이다마는 택시가 잘 있더나 어데?」

하긴 그렇기도 하리라고 그는 생각하였다.

모처럼 발걸음을 한 경우에도 노인은 그의 곁에서 두 밤을 묵는 때가 드물었다. 하룻밤 새기가 무섭게 부진부진 나서곤 했던 것이다. 그가 때로는 역정을 섞어 만류해보지만 매양 부질없는 짓이었다.

「아이다, 어서 가봐야 된다. 약속도 있고, 멋보담도 내가 없으마 집안 돌아가능 기 잘 안 된다 아이가. 여게 더 있으마 머 할 끼고. 내사 까깝시럽기만 하제. 너거 얼굴 봤으마 됐다. 나는 그마 가볼란다.」

그리고는 기어이 일어서버리곤 하던 노인네였다.

「구들묵에 꿀단지 묻어놓고 오신 모양이지.」그는 일쑤 그렇게 투덜댔고, 아내는 또 아내대로「자식 사랑은 내리사랑이란 말 있잖아요. 아버님은 막내도련님 걱정 땜에 그러시는 거라구요」하는 식으로 이해하려 하였다.

아내 말이 옳을지도 모른다. 막내는 그의 큰아이보다 오히려 세 살이 아래였다. 그의 쪽에서 보자면, 계모에게서 늦게 얻은 동생이었다. 그런데, 고2짜리 녀석인데

to the so-called bath culture. His father followed him into the bathhouse halfheartedly, but he wasn't ready at all to go on to taking off his clothes and so on among total strangers. He just stood there awkwardly, looking around left and right. The lenses of the heavy horn-rimmed spectacles, pressing down on his father's fragile bridge, looked all the more foggy. He began taking off his clothes, turning deliberately away from his father.

Before he turned back to the old man, he at last took off his glasses. His eyesight measured zero point something. The fact helped him feel less embarrassed to face his father, to a certain extent. He finally turned around. Then he saw his father struggling to unbutton, reluctantly, his aloha shirt. His fingers moved very clumsily.

"Wait please, Father. Let me do it," he approached his father.

But then, the old man began to back away taking a couple of hesitant steps, saying hastily, "No. I'm good. I'll do it myself."

He waited a while, smiling. The old man's hands were in a greater fluster than before. They kept fumbling with the buttons, which were in fact quite loosely fastened, to no avail. He took a step to-

도 아버지가 집을 비우면 잠을 제대로 자지 못한다는 얘기였다. 노인으로 말하자면, 원래는 자식들에게 데면데면하던 성품이다. 장남인 그부터도, 당신에게서 각별히 사랑받은 기억 같은 건 남아 있지 않다. 그런 사실과 견주어본다면 막내 녀석에 관한 한 아내의 지적이 썩 옳을 수도 있겠다고 그는 고개를 끄덕이곤 했었다.

모든 생명체는 더 많은 자기 개체를 만들기 위해 대부분의 에너지를 탕진한다고 누가 그랬던가? 그가 아내와 자주 하는 농담이 있다. 당신과 내가 만나서 1남 1녀를 두었으니 그것만으로도 본전치기 인생은 되는 것 아니냐는 게 그것이었다. 그렇다면 아버지는 톡톡히 흑자 인생이라고 그는 생각한다. 두 여자에게서 자그마치 8남매를 두었으니까 말이다.

「내 지금 죽어도 벨로 한시럽을 끼 없다.」

언젠가 당신이 하시던 말이다. 「그저 쟈 하나가 쪼매 마음에 걸리기는 한다만서도……」

그때도 당신은 역시 막내를 걱정하셨던 것이다. 하지만 녀석도 이제는 어린애가 아니다. 덩치는 오히려, 날로 쪼그라들고 있는 아버지보다 더 크고 튼실하다. 노인네가 아들을 걱정할 것이 아니라 녀석이 되레 늙은

wards the old man again.

"See? Father, you need a secretary to follow you around, now."

"Among us old people, a secretary is known to mean a walking stick, did you know that?" his father laughed along. "I think I need a stick to walk around with now."

The old man continued, "Walking isn't so bad. But getting in and out of the car is hard. All the more so with them buses. The driver honks on and on, urging me to get off quickly. My knees knock together bad, my head spins. My goodness, by the time I get off the bus, my back is wet and sticky in a sweat."

"If possible, Father, don't take the bus any more. It's dangerous for seniors."

"What should I take then?"

"The taxi, of course."

"What're you talking about? It's expensive, for one, but worst of all, it's not easy to get a taxi, is it?"

He agreed with his father on that point.

Even on his rare visits, the old man seldom stayed longer than one night at his place. At the crack of dawn the next day of his arrival, his father

아버지를 걱정해야 할 판인 것이다. 이제는 그 점을 당신도 좀 깨달아주었으면 좋겠다고 그는 늘상 안타까워하였다. 그래야 이쪽저쪽을 자유롭게 오가며 만년을 보낼 수 있을 게 아닌가. 일흔 고개를 넘어선 지금에서 그런 것에 묶여 있다는 사실이 그를 때로는 답답하게 만드는 것이었다. 적어도 임종만은 내 집에서 맞았으면 하고 그는 소망하였다.

노인네의 마음을 붙잡아 매는 것이 어찌 막내뿐이랴. 그와 동복의 형제들은, 어쩌다보니 죄다 서울로 올라와 있었다. 서로 기댈 만하다거나 또는 그러자고 죽이 맞아 돌아간 것도 아닌데 어느새 그렇게 돼 있었던 것이다. 결국 대구 바닥에는 시집간 누나들과 그리고, 계모 소생의 동생들만 남았다. 여자야 출가외인이랬으니 논외로 하고 보면, 참 공교롭게도 편을 가른 꼴이었다. 노인의 나들이는 그러므로 그 두 쪽을 넘나드는 일이어서 항용 껄쩍지근한 분위기 같은 것을 묻어들이고 또 묻혀가게 마련이었다. 그래서 늘 조심스럽기도 하였다.

사실이 그랬다. 노인의 상경은 언제나 느닷없고 예사롭지 못하였다. 나중에 드러나게 마련이지만, 거기에는 반드시 갈등이 숨어 있곤 하였는데 그것은 대개의 경우

would insist on leaving for home. Of course, he'd tried to hold the old man back, but it had always been useless.

"No. I've got to go back. I've an appointment to keep, and most of all, nothing's run smoothly over there without me, you know. Besides, I've nothing to do here. I'll just get bored. I'm happy now that I've seen your faces, so I'm leaving."

Then, the old man would get up and be gone quickly.

"He must have a precious jar of honey hidden somewhere back home," he'd always complain; and then his wife would say, "You know the saying, 'Love runs one-way from older to younger.' Father's just worried about your youngest brother," tying to understand the old man in her own way.

His wife may have been right. His youngest brother was three years younger than his first son. It was his half-brother his father and stepmother had later in the old man's life. The problem was, the brother, a junior in high school, couldn't sleep well at night without having his father at home. The old man had been rather indifferent to his children, especially the older ones. He, as the firstborn, had no memory of being particularly loved by his fa-

계모와의 사이에서 빚어진 것이었다. 노인의 나들이는 결국 가출에 해당하는 셈이었다. 말하자면 계모에 대한, 나약한 노인네의 시위였다. 계모는 아버지에 비해 젊고 성품도 괄괄한 편이었다. 두 분 사이에는 이래저래 마찰이 잦은 모양이었다. 노인네는, 참을 만큼 참고 속으로 삭이다가 정 못 견딜 정도가 되면 저 낡은 비닐백에다 옷가지 몇 점 챙겨 들고 훌쩍 집을 나서는 것이었다. 여기 아니라도 의탁할 데 얼마든지 있다는 것을 직접 보여주는 셈이었다. 그리고 그 점에서라면 효과만점의 제스처이기도 하였다. 대부분의 경우 항복신호가 시외전화를 통해 그 즉시로 날아들곤 했기 때문이다. 그러면 노인은 또, 날이 새기가 바쁘게 귀갓길에 오르곤 하였다. 상경할 때의 그 풀죽은 모습과는 달리, 이번에는 아주 활기에 차서 말이다.

남방을 벗고 나자 이번에는 바지의 혁대가 말썽을 부리는 눈치였다. 골마리가 삐죽이 빠져나올 정도로 느슨히 매어졌는데도 불구하고 노인은 그것과 한참이나 실랑이를 하였다. 결국 그의 도움을 받아서야 간신히 풀었다.

「오다가 길에서 하나 사맸디마는 억시게 **빡빡하네**.

ther. Taking that into consideration, he couldn't help but nod in agreement with his wife, as far as his youngest brother was concerned.

Who is it that said every living organism uses up most of its energy in creating as many copies of itself as possible? There was a joke about it he and his wife often repeated: Actually, they had at least recovered their investment by producing one son and one daughter. Seen from that point of view, his father had managed his life pretty much in the black, since he had produced as many as 8 sons and daughters with two different women.

"I've nothing to complain about even if I died right now," his father had once said, "It's just that child that I'm a bit worried about..."

It was indeed his youngest brother that his father was talking about even at the time. However, the old man's youngest son was no longer a child. He was bigger and more solidly built than his father who had been dwindling in size over the years. Honestly, the old man shouldn't have worried about his son; rather, the son should have worried for his aged father. It was about time his father came to accept the truth, he often thought in frustration. The old man should be able to spend the

소가죽이라 카디마는 차말로 그렁갑제?」

노인은 뽑아든 혁대를 새삼스레 들여다보며 감탄하였다.

「진짜 소가죽인지 어떤지는 모르겠습니다마는 허리띠가 이렇게 억세어서야 쓰겠어요 어디. 부드러운 걸로 이따 바꿉시다.」

그는 대꾸하며 고소지었다.

「세월이 가마 부드럽으진다 아이가.」

노인이, 무슨 쓸데없는 소리냐는 듯이 강변하였다.「4천 원이나 주고 산 긴데 그라마 기양 냅비릴 끼가? 좀 뻑시기는 해도 얼매나 찔기겠노. 내 죽을 때꺼정 허리띠 걱정은 안 해도 되겠다 아이가.」

이쪽을 기웃거리는 시선들이 있었기 때문에 그는 그 대단한 쇠가죽 허리띠에 대해서는 더 이상의 언급을 자제하였다. 그는, 노인이 내의를 마저 벗기를 잠자코 기다렸다가 맨 마지막으로 양말을 벗겨드렸다. 마침내 완전히 알몸들이 되었다. 두 부자는 잠시 마주 서서 서로의 모습을 건네다보았다. 이상하게도 가슴이 뭉클해지는 순간을 그는 경험하였다.

그는 노인의 한쪽 팔을 잡고 탕으로 들어갔다.

rest of his life going back and forth freely between Daegu and Seoul. At times, he was baffled by the fact that his father was still tied down like that even when he was over seventy. He wished that he could wait at his father's deathbed at his apartment.

And also, his youngest brother was not the only one that was pulling at his father's heartstrings. All of his male siblings who shared the same mother happened to live in Seoul. Not that they'd planned to ahead of time since they got along well or wanted to help one another; it was just that by the time they realized it, all of them had already been settled down in Seoul. In the end, the only siblings still living in Daegu were the married sisters on his mother's side and the younger ones on his stepmother's. Putting the married sisters aside, as the old saying goes, "Married daughters are outsiders," the family was, as it happened, divided into two sides as if by design. The old man's outings were like crossing the boundary to and fro; so there was something like an aura of leeriness that was persistently brought in and out by the old man on his comings and goings. So, they all tried to be careful all the time.

As a matter of fact, his father's visit to Seoul was

「조심하세요. 바닥이 미끄러워요.」

자욱한 수증기 속을 헤치고 들어가면서 그는 노인에게 주의를 드렸다. 마르고 굽은 두 다리가 마치 얼음판 위를 가듯 불안하게 더듬고 있었다.

부모 자식 간에는 어딘가 반드시 닮게 마련이라는 사실은 매우 당연하면서도 새삼스럽게 희한한 느낌을 주는 경우가 더러 있는 법이다. 그들 부자를 두고 주변 사람들이 자주 그런 걸 느끼는 모양이었다. 참 어쩌면 싶게 서로 닮은 점이 많다는 지적들이었다. 속없는 웃음이 그렇고, 시력이 나쁜 게 그렇고, 마르고 꺼부정한 체격이 그렇고, 허청허청 걷는 걸음걸이가 그렇고, 무엇엔가 몰두하거나 잠깐 방심하고 있을 때의 그 멍한 표정이 또 그렇다는 식이었다. 그의 아내는 때문에 곧잘 웃음을 터뜨리고는 하였다. 두 부자를 앞세우고 길을 나서다 말고 뒤에서 혼자 끼들끼들 웃는 경우가 흔히 있는데 그럴 때 핀잔을 주면 대꾸가 이랬다.

「두 분 뒷모습이 너무너무 같아요. 꺼부정하게 굽은 허리 하며 힘없는 걸음걸이, 게다가 뒷머리 곱슬거리는 것까지요. 어떻게 웃지 않고 배길 수가 있나요?」

그리고는 한바탕 깔깔댄 다음 또 이렇게 덧붙이는 것

always unexpected and unnatural. As it turned out, each of the visits was, without exception, provoked by a conflict, mostly with his stepmother. The old man's outing amounted to, as it were, running away from home. In other words, it was the protest of a fragile old man against his second wife. She was much younger than the old man and rather quick-tempered. There seemed to be frequent quarrels between them over this and that. The old man would try to be patient as long as he could; and when he couldn't deal with it anymore, he would toss some clothes in that old vinyl bag of his and just take off. It was to show that he had other places to go where he could be taken care of. In that respect, it was a perfectly effective gesture, since ten to one he would get a long-distance call of surrender from his wife right away. Then the old man would be on his way back home at the crack of dawn. Unlike his dispirited self arriving in Seoul, he would be full of life when leaving for Daegu.

After taking off the shirt, the old man began struggling with his belt this time. The belt was fastened so loosely that the waist of his trousers had slipped off of it; and yet, the old man spent quite some time tugging and picking at it. Eventually,

이었다.「절대루 제 잘못이 아니라구요. 이웃 여자들도 다 그런다구요, 정말. 아버님이랑 당신이랑 석이랑 그렇게 3대가 나란히 길을 나설 때면 동네사람들이 뭐래는지 아세요? 저건 작품이다 작품! 그런다구요 글쎄……」

어느 정도 사실에 근거하고 있는지는 모를 노릇이나 흔히 전하는 말로, 호랑이는 특히 고양이를 싫어한다고들 한다. 이유인즉슨 자기 모습을 너무 많이 닮았기 때문이라는 것이다. 그러고 보면 아들 석이에 대한 자신의 심리 저변에도 혹 그런 요소가 있는지 모를 일이라고 그는 가끔 생각해온 터였다. 일테면 녀석에게서 심약하거나 소극적인 태도 같은 것이 눈에 띌 때 그는 매번 불같은 노여움을 드러내고는 하였는데, 그런 결함이야말로 바로 자신의 것이면서 또 아버지의 것이라고 믿어지는 까닭에서였다. 그가 이 나이까지 살아오면서 이것만은 결단코 아버지를 닮지 말아야겠다고 이를 악물어온 것이 있다면 그게 바로 아버지의 저 겁 많고 소극적인 인생 태도였던 것이다.

물론 당신이 살아온 세월은 고난의 연속이었다. 그것을 모르는 바가 아니었다. 아버지는 3·1만세사건이 있

only with his help was his father able to unfasten the belt.

"I bought it on my way from a street vender. Gosh, it sure is stiff! It must be genuine leather as the vender says."

The old man admired the belt in his hands, taking a closer look at it.

"I'm not sure if it's genuine leather or not, but a belt shouldn't be that stiff. Let's get a soft one later."

He said, smiling bitterly.

"It'll become softer over time, won't it?"

The old man insisted stubbornly, as if to say he would stand no nonsense. "I've paid 4,000 *won* for it. Are you telling me to just throw it away? It's a bit tough, but think about how long it'll last? Now, I don't need to worry about belts as long as I live. See what I mean?"

Noticing some heads turning toward him and his father, he refrained from talking about that fine genuine leather belt any further. He waited without saying another word for the old man to strip off his underwear and then, helped him remove his socks. At last, both of them were naked. The father and son stood there face to face for a while, looking at each other. Curiously enough, for a moment he felt

었던 바로 그 기미생이다. 따라서 암흑의 일제 말을 거쳐 20대 중반에 해방을 맞았지만 곧 동족상잔의 저 끔찍한 선쟁의 폭풍 속으로 말려들고 만다. 그리고 휴전—저 50년대의 궁핍한 삶으로 이어지는 것이다. 우리가 그나마 굶지 않고 밥술이라도 뜰 수 있게 된 것이 언제부터이던가? 흔히 말하듯이 지난 70년대부터라고 한다면 그때는 이미 당신의 생애는 파장에 이르고 있었던 셈이다. 어언, 환갑을 눈앞에 둔 신세였으니까 말이다.

그렇다고는 하더라도 그로서는 도무지 잊혀지지 않는, 그래서 불쑥불쑥 떠오를 때마다 아직도 당신을 바라보는 눈이 결코 순해지지 못하는, 참으로 아프고 어두운 기억들이 남아 있었다. 어느 해던가의 정월 대보름날이었다. 전후의 궁핍 속에서도 명절은 역시 명절이었다. 이웃들은 가난하나마 그래도 오곡밥을 서로 나누었고, 아이들은 공터로 몰려다니며 쥐불을 놓느라고 떠들썩하였다. 그러나 그의 식구들만은 예외였다. 고향을 버리고 이웃 도시 대구로 옮겨 앉은 지 얼마 되지 않던 때였다. 단칸 셋방에서 문을 닫아건 채 그의 식구들은 하루 종일 꼼짝달싹도 하지 않았던 것이다. 사정을 모를 리 없는 주인댁이 아침결에 슬며시 디밀어준 잡곡밥

a lump in the throat.

He led the old man by his arm to the bathroom.

"Please, be careful. The floor's slippery." As they walked through the thick steam, he cautioned the old man. The old man's thin, bowed legs moved uneasily, as if they were groping their way on ice.

Naturally, children are bound to resemble their parents in one way or another; and yet, that fact may flabbergast others when the level of likeness is extreme. The people around the old man and his son often seemed to find it absolutely uncanny when they saw them together. They pointed out a number of father-son resemblances: their innocent laughter, poor eyesight, thin physique, slouching posture, shambling walk, and vacant expression when they were absent-minded or engrossed in something, and so forth. Their resemblances often made his wife burst out laughing. For instance, whenever the couple and the old man were on their way out together, his wife would look at the father and son walking side by side ahead of her and begin giggling. When he talked to her about it one day, she answered:

"The two of you look so much alike from behind. Your stooped backs, sluggish walk, and even the

한 그릇이 머리맡에서 줄기차게 냄새를 풍기고 있었지만 아무도 손대지 않았다. 시체들처럼 내처 이불을 들쓰고 해종일 드러누워 있기만 했던 것이다. 차라리 배고픔은 참을 만하였다. 난처한 것은 요의였다. 화장실에 가자면 만부득이 문 밖을 나서야만 하였고, 또 줄줄이 늘어서 있는 여러 개의 방문 앞을 지나가야만 하였다. 평소에는 아무렇지도 않던 그 일이 그날만은 왜 그렇게나 끔찍할 만큼 부끄럽고 창피하게 생각되었는지! 참다 참다 못해 기어이 문을 열고 나섰을 때는 너무나 분한 나머지 눈물을 질끔거렸던 것이다. 뒤꼭지에 따갑게 와 닿는 이웃들의 시선을 헤치고 그 굴욕스러운 장소에서 돌아온 그는 다시 이불 속으로 기어들기 전에 아버지 쪽을 잔뜩 꼬누어 내려다보았었다. 그때처럼 아버지가 원망스러웠던 적은 다시없었다. 당신은 벽을 향해 길게 드러누운 채 죽은 사람처럼 미동도 하지 않았다. 식구들을 기아와 치욕 속에다 팽개쳐둔 채 당신이 할 수 있는 능력이 오직 그것뿐인 듯 줄기차게—단 한 번도 문 밖 출입을 하지 않은 채 참으로 줄기차게—드러누워 있기만 했던 것이다. 어린 마음에도 침을 뱉고 싶었었다고 그는 또렷이 기억한다.

curly hair on the back of your heads. I can't help laughing about it!"

And then she had another good cackle over it before she added:

"It's not my fault at all. The ladies in the neighborhood all say the same thing, I swear. Do you know what our neighbors say when they see Father, you, and Sok-i, the three generations walking side by side? 'That's a work of art, definitely, a real work of art!' That's what they say, you know..."

No one knows to what extent it's based on the truth, but people say that tigers don't like cats. It is because cats resemble tigers too much. If so, he thought occasionally, deep down in his own mentality towards his son Sok-i, he harbored something similar to that animal instinct. For example, whenever he noticed weak-mindedness or a passive attitude in his son, he suddenly found himself enraged, perhaps, because he believed that the defect had run from his father to him and then to his son. If there was one thing that he had been trying, gritting his teeth, all his life not to take after his father, it was none other than *that* cowardly and passive attitude towards life.

Of course, his father's life had been a long series

그리고 또, 그 몇 해 뒤다. 그의 가정은 변함없이 가난 속에서 허덕이고 있었다. 어쩌자고 이번에는 그의 몸이 병을 얻었다. 감기거니 했던 것이 한 달여나 끌더니 마침내는 의식이 수시로 가물가물해지기에 이르고 만 것이었다. 피골이 상접해진 그를 끌어안고 식구들은 안타까워했지만 그러나 대책은 전무하였다. 보다 못한 이웃들이, 어떡하든 아이는 살려놓고 봐야 할 게 아니냐고, 그러자면 무작정 병원으로 떠메고 들어가 입원부터 시켜놓고 볼 일이라고 이구동성으로 충고하였다. 그러나 그때도 아버지는 그런 식이었다. 떠메고 들어간다고 받아준다더냐, 혹 입원은 했다 쳐도 그 뒷감당은 누가 할 거냐고, 당신은 시종 쓴 입만 다셨던 것이다. 자주 가물거리는 의식 속에서도 그는 아버지에 대한 혐오감을 참을 길이 없었다. 나중에야 누나가 전해준 얘기지만, 마침내 그는 고열 속에서 의식을 완전히 잃어버린 채 아버지를 향해 마구 욕설을 퍼대기까지 했다는 것이었다. 지금도 그때의 이야기만 나오면 누님은 곧잘 웃고는 한다.

「야, 니 그때 차말로 무섭더래이. 아부지한테 막 퍼대는데 아이고, 누가 그기 어린아라카겠더노. 너거마 살라카나, 나는 죽어도 갠찮나 어짜고 그카는데 앗다 마

of hardships. Not that he wasn't aware of it. His father was born in 1919, the year of *kimi* when the March First *Manse* Demonstrations for National Independence took place. He grew up in the dark age of the Japanese colonial occupation of Korea, and witnessed the nation's liberation in his mid-twenties, only to be embroiled soon into the storm of the horrible internecine war between the North and the South Koreans. Then, the armistice—the beginning of the period of abject poverty, which continued throughout the 1950s. When was it that we as a nation began to rise above starvation? If the answer was the 1970s, as it was generally known, by then his father had already reached the closing years of his life. That is, the old man was pushing sixty.

Be that as it may, as for him, there were excruciating and dismal memories that he could never forget and therefore could never look at his father with sympathy, whenever he had flashbacks. It happened on the first full moon day of January, one year. Even in poverty after the Korean War, a festive day was still a festive day. Neighbors, poor as they were, shared the five-grain rice; and children milled about, clamoring, from one vacant lot

내가 다 씩껍 묵었다카이!」

　매사에 겁이 많고 그리고 소극적인 태도—그것은 확실히 족보에 있는 것이라고 그는 생각한다. 그런 성품을 대물림하지 않으려고 스스로 이를 악물고 안간힘 해왔지만 그러나 뒤돌아보면 그저 얼굴이 붉어지기만 할 따름인 것이다. 아들 녀석인 석이에게서 그런 요소를 발견함은 차라리 당연하다고 해야 하리라. 그럼에도 불구하고 매번 불같이 치미는 화증을 스스로 억제하기가 어려운 것은 또 어찌된 노릇인가? 그에 비긴다면 외모가 닮는 거야 무슨 상관이랴. 그런 따위야 아무래도 무관하다고 그는 생각하는 것이었다.

　「참 희한해요. 당신하고 석이는 손톱 발톱 모양까지 흡사하다구요. 난 헛건가 뵈, 두 애들한테 한 군데도 닮은 구석을 찾을 수가 없으니 원.」

　언젠가 아내가 하던 말을 그는 또 기억해냈다. 정말 그럴까? 노인은 탕 속에서 나와 타일 바닥 위에 웅크리고 앉았다. 열탕에서 한동안 익힌 터라 피부가 검붉게 익어 있었다. 노인네들의 벗은 몸을 볼 때마다 늘 느끼는 것이지만, 무엇보다 눈에 띄는 것은 균형감의 상실이었다. 몸이 비대한 사람은 비대한 대로 또 마른 사람

to another, setting the rat-chasing fire to the dry fields.

However, his family was the only exception. It was not so long after they left their hometown and moved to the neighboring city, Daegu. In the single room they rented, his family locked themselves in all day, never taking a single step out of their room. The owner of the rental house, who of course knew their situation, quietly slipped a bowl of five-grain rice into their room in the morning; but no one even touched the bowl of rice that sat at the head of their beds as it filled the room with its delicious smell. Like corpses, they lay in bed all day long with the quilts pulled over themselves.

He was able, in fact, to endure his hunger. What really embarrassed him, however, was the call of nature. In order to go to the toilet, he had no choice but to leave the room and walk along the corridor lined with doors. He usually thought nothing of it; but on that day, what a horribly embarrassing and humiliating task that was! When he couldn't stand it anymore and had to get out of the room, tears stood in his eyes out of a sense of mortification. After walking back from his disgrace and back to his room, feeling the stinging eyes of

은 마른 대로 한결같이 어딘가 균형이 무너져 있게 마
련이던 것이다. 당신은 비쩍 마르고 긴 사지에 비해 아
랫배가 별나게 튀어나온 편이었다. 게다가 왼쪽 어깨가
눈에 띄게 내려앉은 상태였다. 당신은 평생을 가난 속
에서 살아왔지만, 그렇다고 심하게 막노동을 한 편은
아니었다. 그럼에도 불구하고 육체는 속절없이 균형을
잃고, 허무하게 무너지고, 그리고 무참히 짜부라져 있
었다. 그는 한동안 말없이 그것을 보고 있었다. 무형의,
갈퀴 같은 손이 보이는 듯싶었다. 그 손이, 당신의 육체
가 끝까지 쇠잔하기를 기다렸다가 마침내 마른 검불처
럼 쓸어가리라. 눈 속에 모래를 집어넣은 것처럼 깔깔
하였다.

　그는 때밀이 타월을 집어 들고 노인에게 다가갔다. 그
리고는 검붉게 익어 있는 노인의 등을 밀기 시작하였
다. 뼈 마디마디가 손바닥에 아프게 느껴졌다. 놀랍도
록 잔약한 느낌이어서 도대체 그 험한 세월을 어떻게
버티어왔는지가 의심스러울 지경이었다. 발을 내려다
보았다. 그것은 타일 바닥 위에 마른 나무토막처럼 방
치되어 있었다. 그는 얼른 자신의 발과 대조해보았다.
그리고는 혼자 고소하였다. 엄지와 검지의 생긴 모양이

his neighbors on the back of his head all the way, he cast a venomous stare down at his father for a long while before he crawled back into bed. He had never experienced that much of a grudge against his father before or after. His father lay facing the wall, like a dead body, not stirring at all. With his entire family cast down in the midst of starvation and humiliation, his father just lay there—not ever leaving the room once—as if that was all he could manage to do. He still vividly remembered, merely a child as he was back then, how he wanted to spit in the face of his useless father.

That was not all. Even several years later, his family was still struggling. This time, he suddenly fell ill. At first, they all thought it was just a common cold, but when it dragged on over a month, he ended up losing consciousness on and off. Holding the child, all skin and bones, in their arms, his family was in turmoil, but there was nothing they could do. The neighbors, who couldn't ignore the situation any longer, suggested unanimously that they should just carry the boy into the hospital and get him admitted first. Even then, however, his father was what he was.

"Do you think they'll take him in, even if we force

며 구부러진 형태가 참 어쩌면 싫게 흡사하였던 것이다.

「대강 해라 그마.」

성가신 듯 노인이 말하였다. 가느다란 두 다리를 꺾어 가슴 앞에 끌어안고 등을 활처럼 휘게 웅크린 채였다. 너무 작고 가벼운 느낌이어서 그는 등 뒤에서 두 팔로 노인을 싸안고 가만히 들어올려보았다. 허무할 만큼 체중이 없었다. 그때 노인이 또 말하였다.

「남들은 몸이 자꼬 뿔어서 걱정이라카더라마는 내사 맨날 그기 그거라. 노인네가 너무 말라도 초라해 뵌다꼬 할마시는 덜 좋아한다카이.」

할마시란 계모를 가리키는 말이었다.

「뭘요, 고령자일수록 체중이 덜 나가는 게 좋답니다. 몸이 나는 것보다는 마르고 또 변동이 없어야 된대요. 그래야 장수한답니다.」

노인은 잠시 헛웃음을 웃었다. 「씰데없이 오래 살마 머 할 끼고, 백죄 지 고롭고 남 귀찮구로!」

그리고는, 다시 예의 웃음을 길게 이었다. 결코 빈말 같지만은 않은 느낌이었다.

상상외로 노인의 몸에서는 때가 많이 나왔다. 하긴 당연한 노릇이다, 하고 그는 생각하였다. 당신에게 목욕

our way into the hospital carrying the boy like this? Let's just say that they take him in. Who's going to take care of the bills?" his father just kept clicking his tongue bitterly.

Even while his consciousness flickered in and out, he couldn't suppress his hatred for his father. He heard all about it only later from his older sister: When he became delirious with a high fever, he even began heaping abuses on his father. His sister always laughed whenever they talked about that time:

"You really frightened us at the time. Cursing and swearing at Father, my goodness, who would have said it was just a child who was doing it? 'You don't care if I die or not, as long as you still live, do you?' and so on. That's what you said. Good lord, I was scared to death!"

Timid and passive in everything—he knew it was in his blood. He had made every effort not to inherit the disposition himself, but looking back, he only found himself blushing in shame. It was only natural that he should notice the same personality traits in his son Sok-i. Why, then, was it so difficult for him to suppress his fury each time he saw it in his son? Who cares if we look alike? Regarding

탕은 여전히 별난 장소일 테니까 말이다. 화장실만큼이나 무시로 출입하는 일상공간은 못 되는 것이다. 도대체 1년에 몇 번 정도나 발길을 들여놓을까. 아직도 당신의 의식 속에는 설대목이나 무슨 특별한 때 찾는 곳쯤으로 굳어 있는지도 모른다. 그는 어렸을 때 아버지와 함께 목욕탕을 다닌 기억들을 떠올렸다. 주로 노동회관에 있는 목욕탕을 다녔었다. 일반 목욕탕보다는 요금이 훨씬 쌌기 때문에 시설이 그만큼 후지고, 그리고 또 언제나 만원이었다. 전쟁이 끝난 지도 대여섯 해가 지난 50년대 후반, 세상살이가 여전히 각박하던 무렵이었다. 그래서였는지도 모른다. 몸을 씻는 일도 전쟁이란 기분이 실감 날정도로 거기서는 일쑤 아귀다툼을 벌여야만 하였다. 누구나 일단 들어갔나 하면 난난히 밑천을 뽑은 후에야 나왔다. 땀을 뻘뻘 흘리면서 열심히 씻고 씻고 또 씻고, 나중에는 손이며 발등 같은 데서 피가 나도록 껍질을 벗겨낸 다음에야 비로소 그 연옥과도 같은 욕탕에서 시뻘건 몸뚱어리를 빼내가는 것이었다. 하지만 당신은 거기서도 별로 악착스럽지 못하였다고 그는 기억한다. 뒷전으로 내몰린 채 잠시 어물거리다가 그만 나가버리곤 했던 것이다. 말하자면 그것이, 세상을 사

physical resemblances, he didn't care either one way or the other.

"It's really unbelievable. You and Sok-i look alike even in fingernails and toenails. It seems as though I had no part in it. I share no features with either one of our children, none whatsoever."

He reminded himself of yet another remark his wife had made one day. Was it true? he wondered. The old man left the bathtub and crouched down on the tiled floor. His father's skin was red all over after soaking himself in the hot water for a while. Whenever he saw the naked body of an old man, the first thing he noticed was the loss of balance. Whether they were fleshy or thin, old men were bound to have lost balance in one part or another of their body. His father was very thin. He had long arms and legs, and oddly, had a potbelly. More-over, his left shoulder was visibly sunken. Although his father had lived his whole life in poverty, he had never done much hard labor. Nonetheless, his body had inevitably lost its balance, hopelessly collapsed and tragically shrunken. He looked at his father for a while. Then, he thought he saw an in-visible, rake-like hand. That hand would wait until his father's body failed, and sweep him away in the

는 당신의 자세였다.

「목욕탕 좀 자주 다니세요.」

등을 밀다가 내친김에 그는 불쑥 말하였다. 「노인네들은 특히나 자주 다녀야 됩니다. 요새 목욕비 얼마나 쌉니까. 천 원짜리 한 장이면 되잖아요. 일과처럼 매일 다니는 노인들도 많아요.」

사실이 그랬다. 특히 동네 목욕탕은 평일엔 노인들이 대부분이었다. 그는 새삼스레 고개를 쳐들고 주위를 둘러보기까지 하였다. 그리고는 목소리를 낮추어 계속하였다.

「보세요, 전부 그런 노인네들이지요? 거의가 날마다 소일삼아 오는 분들입니다. 요즘 천 원짜리 한 장 가지고 어디 간들 여기보다 더 편하게 시간 보낼 데가 있나요. 저쪽 휴게실에는 테레비도 있고 장기 바둑판 같은 것도 있어 소일하기 그만입니다. 아버진 장기 두는 거 좋아하시잖아요? 이제부턴 목욕탕 자주 드나드는 습관 붙이세요. 나이 드실수록 깨끗하게 하고 다니셔야지 안 그러면 젊은 사람들이 싫어합니다.」

처음 하는 소리가 아니다. 서울 나들이를 오실 때마다 그가 짜증스럽게 되풀이했던 소리였다. 때로는 남 보기

end, as if to rake away dry grass. His eyes burned a little as if sand had gotten in them.

He went over to the old man, a scrubbing towel in his hand. He began to scrub the old man's dark-red back. The old man's bones were painfully evident in his palm. The old man's body felt so fragile that he wondered how on earth he had persisted through all the turbulent times. He looked down at his father's feet. They were carelessly splayed on the floor like two dried-up sticks. He made a quick comparison with his own feet. Then he smiled bitterly to himself. Their big toes and second toes looked so identical in shape and crookedness that he couldn't but marvel at the resemblance.

"That's good enough."

The old man sounded annoyed. He sat with his back crouched like a bow, his knees bent, and his arms hugging his knees. He seemed so small and light that he put his arms around the old man from behind and carefully lifted him up. The old man weighed almost nothing, making him feel empty all of a sudden. Then the old man said:

"Other people complain about getting fatter, but my weight has always been the same. Granny doesn't like it. She says old people look shabby

민망할 정도로 초라한 모습이곤 했기 때문이다. 거기다 노인 특유의 냄새 같은 게 있어 심할 땐 그의 아이들조차 슬슬 피하는 경우가 없지 않았다. 하지만 노인네는 도무지 귀담아듣지 않았다. 당신 말인즉 그게 편하다는 것이었다. 아무리 역정을 내도 마찬가지였다. 저 속 좋은 웃음만 흘릴 따름이던 것이다.

그러던 분이 어쩐 셈인지 이번에는 대꾸가 좀 달랐다. 「그라기는 해야 되겠제? 할마시도 이래 나서는 거 보마 질색하는 기라. 말이사 맞제. 그기 마이 옳다카이. 늙은 이한테는 와, 안 좋은 냄새 같응 기 안 있나. 열차 칸 같은 데서도 노인들 옆자리는 사람들이 잘 안 앉을라카대. 팽상 우리 겉은 늙다리끼리 몰키앉는 기라. 그기 우리덜도 핀코…… 말 마래이. 늙으마 차말로 섧다카이. 식당 같은 데서는 더 그렇다 아이가. 똥을 옆에 놓고 묵으마 묵었지, 늙은이들하고는 같이 몬 묵겠다카는 기라.」

노인네는 오히려 유쾌하다는 듯이 소리 내어 한참을 웃었다. 그도 가만히 따라 웃었다. 열탕 속에 몸을 푹 담근 채 시조 가락 같은 것을 흥얼흥얼 읊조리고 있던 노인과, 타일 바닥에다 타월을 깔고 반듯하게 드러누워

when they're too thin."

By Granny, the old man meant his stepmother.

"As a matter of fact, losing weight is better for older people than gaining weight. Being thin and keeping the same weight, I've heard these two are the secret to a long life," the son said.

The old man simpered. "What's the point of living a long time anyways? Hard on yourself and hard on the people around you!"

And then, the old man feigned a laugh again, only longer this time. It didn't sound like a mere passing remark, though.

The old man had much more dirt and grime on his body than he had expected. Wasn't it to be expected, though? To his father, the public bathhouse was still a special place. It wasn't an everyday space like washrooms where he could go whenever he needed to. *How many times does he visit the bathhouse a year at any rate?* he wondered. Perhaps, in his father's mind, it still remained as a place where he could go only on special occasions like the New Year season. He recalled the days of his childhood when he visited public bathhouses with his father. Most of the time, it was the one located in the Labor Hall. Admission was much cheaper

있던 다른 노인이 잠시 이쪽을 기웃거렸다. 말귀를 대충은 알아들은 표정들이었다. 그러나 화제가 도무지 달갑지 않은 듯 짐짓 외면들을 하였다. 탕 속의 노인은 기분이 언짢아지기라도 한 모양이었다. 시조 가락을 멈추고는 아주 과장되게 불쾌한 표정을 지었다.

그는 잠시 얼굴을 붉혔다. 묵묵히 고개를 떨군 채 이번에는 노인의 팔을 끌어다 정성들여 밀기 시작하였다. 왼쪽 겨드랑이 바로 아래켠에 길쭉하게 드러나 있는 흉터가 눈에 띄었다. 이게 바로 그거구나! 그는 혼자 중얼댔다. 아주 까맣게 잊어버렸던 어릴 적 친구와 길거리에서 우연히 맞닥뜨린 것 같은, 흡사 그런 감회가 가슴을 뭉클하게 만들었다. 그것은 총상 자국이었다. 자칫하면 치명적인 것이 될 법했던, 그리하여 한 사내의 생애를 일찌감치 끝장내게 했을지도 모를, 바로 그 작고 당돌한 쇠붙이의 흔적이었다. 그리고 그것은 또 당신의 몸에 기록된 한 시대의 부호이기도 하다고, 그는 새삼스러운 감개에 젖었다. 전쟁 막바지에, 그것도 길거리에서 끌려간 지 불과 석 달하고 닷새 만에 당한 일이라고 했었다. 상처가 제대로 아물기도 전에 귀가하였던 그해 여름만 해도 보기가 끔찍스러울 정도로 큰 상처였

there than at other regular ones. Naturally, its facilities were that much inferior, and it was always crowded. Even in the latter half of the 1950s, five or six years after the end of the war, it was still difficult to make a living in the country. Perhaps that's why little battles constantly going on inside the bathhouse, to the point that it seemed like bathing was a war in itself. Once inside, no one would leave until they all felt that they had truly got what they had paid for it. They all washed and washed, sweating profusely, until the back of their hands and feet were scrubbed to the point of bleeding. Only then would they take their raw bodies out of that Purgatory of the bathhouse. His father, however, was hardly dogged enough even inside the bathhouse, as far as he could remember. He and his father were driven to the margins and went through the motions of washing, before they left the place. In a nutshell, that was his father's attitude towards life.

"Father, you should come to the bathhouse more often."

As he scrubbed his father's back, he blurted out, having decided that he might as well say it then while he was at it. "Old people especially should

었다. 그러나 청사에 기록된 문자도 세월에 바래듯이 이제는 흡사 곶감 꼭지처럼 오므라든 채 찌들고 메마르고 오종종한 꼴로 거기 남아 있었다.

그는 그 흉터를 때밀이 타월로 가만히 쓸어보았다. 세상사에 대해 당신이 지나치게 겁이 많고 소심해진 것도 어쩌면 그때부터였는지 모른다는 생각을 그는 문득 품었다. 살아생전 어머니의 푸념도 그랬었다고 기억되었다. 저 냥반은 몸뚱이만 빤하게 돌아온 거지 넋은 전쟁터에 빼놓고 왔다카이. 맨날 구들묵만 짊어지고 있으마 우짜자는 소린지…… 말하자면, 세상 사는 일에 도무지 뜻도 욕심도 없는 양반이라는 비난이었다. 정말 그렇게 불성실한 삶이었던가? 그의 기억으로는 꼭이 그런 것만은 아니었다. 고향을 버리고 이웃 도시 대구로 나앉기 전까지만 해도 아버지는 무언가 새로운 일을 벌여보려고 열심이었던 것이다. 그중에서도 면소재지 마을에다 지방신문 지국을 냈던 일이나 또는, 느닷없이 갓방 두 개를 터서 메리야스 직기를 들여온 일 따위는 지금도 기억에 고스란히 남아 있었다. 당신은 그때만 해도, 40여 가호쯤 되던 고향 마을에서 식자에 속했음 직하다. 그러니까 남들이 변함없이 우직하게 흙과 씨름

take advantage of the facilities as much as they can. It's very cheap these days, isn't it? A thousand *won*, that's all. Many old people now make it part of their daily routine."

It was true. Neighborhood bathhouses, in particular, were occupied mostly by elderly customers on weekdays. He deliberately raised his head and looked around the bathroom. And under his breath, he continued:

"Look, Father, they're all seniors here, you see? Most of them come here everyday to pass their time. What better place can you find nowadays where you can get in and be comfortable on only a thousand *won*. In the resting room over there, there's a TV set and other things like *go* or chess boards, so it's a capital spot to while away some time. Father, you like playing *janggi* chess, don't you? It's time you got into the habit of visiting the bathhouse often. As you get older, you should keep yourself clean and tidy. Otherwise, young people wouldn't like to be around you."

It was not the first time he had ever said that to his father. He'd been peevishly repeating the same thing to his father each time he came to Seoul for a visit. Sometimes, his father would show up in such

할 때도 유독 그런 엉뚱한 일들을 저지를 수 있었던 것이 아닐까. 그것은 확실히 별스런 능력이었을 법도 한 것이다. 낭신이 세상 사는 일에 뜻도 욕심도 잃어버린 채 매사에 겁이 많고 소심해졌으며, 마침내는 대책 없이 무능력한 사람으로 전락해버린 것은 필경 빈손으로 식솔을 끌고 이웃 도시 대구로 옮겨 앉은 이후부터라고 해야 옳으리라. 그날 이래 당신이 제대로 생업을 가져본 적이 있었던가? 도시에서의 삶에서 당신은 그처럼 무능력했었고 그리고 무능력한 만큼 매사 불운하기도 하였다. 그러다 보니 가족의 호구지책은 늘 여자들 손에 맡겨질 수밖에 없었다. 그랬다. 처음엔 어머니에게, 다음엔 누나들에게, 그리고 지금은 계모의 손에 늘 기대온 생애였다고, 그에게는 생각되었다.

노인의 아랫도리를 씻기다가 그는 또 다른 흉터를 찾아냈다. 그것은 오른쪽 넓적다리 바깥쪽에 있었다. 겨드랑이께의 그것보다는 작다고 해도 그 정도 흉터가 남았다면 상처 자체는 상당히 심각했으리라고 짐작되었다. 심하게 노화된 피부임에도 불구하고 터진 자리가 허옇게 드러나 보였다.

「여기 이 상처는 언제 생긴 거지요?」

shabby clothes that he felt embarrassed in front of others. Further, he had a kind of odor typical of the elderly people, so there had been some occasions when the odor became intense, and his children would keep clear of their grandfather. Nevertheless, his father wouldn't listen to his advice. His father insisted that he felt comfortable that way. No matter how angry he got at his father at times, nothing changed. The old man would just keep laughing—that old innocent laugh.

This time, however, for some reason, his father's response was slightly different. "I should, shouldn't I? Granny also hates it when she sees me leaving home dressed like this. You're right. Quite right! Old people *do* have an unpleasant odor on them, don't they? Even on the train, people don't like to sit beside old people. Usually, old people like us end up sitting together. But we also feel comfortable that way... It's beyond words. How sad getting old can be! Especially so in places like restaurants. They say that people would rather eat beside dung if they had to, but not beside old people."

The old man broke out into loud and long laugh, as if he were rather delighted. He quieted down quickly, though. An old man who was sitting in the

때밀이 타월로 그곳을 문지르며 그가 물었다.

「상처라꼬?」

노인이 새삼 고개를 외로 쏘고 내려다보았다.「어데, 그런 기 있나?」

「여기요. 제법 큰 흉턴데요?」

「아, 이거 말이가?」

노인이 손으로 더듬더듬 흉터를 확인하더니 대꾸하였다.「총 맞은 자국 아이가. 육니오사변 때……」

「이거가요?」

그는 반문하였다.「전쟁 때 입은 상처는 이쪽 거잖아요?」

「어데?」

「여기요.」

그는 노인의 손을 끌어다가 겨드랑이께의 흉터를 만져보게 하였다.

「이게 바루 그 총상 자국이잖아요. 눈으로 봐도 알겠는데요, 스쳐지나간 자리가 말입니다. 안 그래요?」

「그러나? 그래 븨나?」

노인의 대답이 어눌해졌다. 갑자기 자신을 잃어버린 목소리였다. 기억을 더듬듯이 노인의 아둔한 손이 흉터

hot water and crooning a *sijo* lyric poem to himself, and another old man who was lying on his back on a towel spread out on the tiled floor—both of them turned their heads to look at him and his father. Their expressions told him that they had overheard them and had a rough idea of what his father had just said. Soon, however, they deliberately looked away, as if the subject wasn't to their taste. The man in the hot-water tub even seemed out of the spirit now. He stopped crooning the *sijo* altogether and his face became long in a quite exaggerated way.

He felt embarrassed for a moment. He bowed his head and pulled one of his father's arms towards him and began scrubbing it with great care. Right under his father's left armpit, a long scar caught his eye.

"Ah, this must be it!" he muttered to himself.

He felt as if he had just run into a long-forgotten childhood friend in the street—a sentiment of the sort went straight to his heart. It was a gunshot wound. It was a trace of that small, bold piece of metal that could end a man's life early. It was also a small trace of an era documented in detail across his father's body, the thought deeply moving him

를 의심스럽게 더듬어보고 있었다. 그리고는 이해할 수 없다는 듯 비뚜름히 고개를 꼬고 한참 생각해보더니 다시 말을 이었다. 역시 자신 없는 말투였다.

「니 말이 맞능 거 겉다. 까딱했으마 갈빗대가 몽창 나갈 뿐했닥고, 니 생모가 늘 그랬디라. 그능어 불콩이 쪼매마 더 우예 됐으마 내사 지금 없지러…… 말도 마라, 그능어 육니오……」

「그래두 영감님은 괜찮시다.」

갑자기 옆에서 참견해왔다. 타일 바닥에 드러누워 있던 노인이었다. 아까부터 이쪽 얘기에 귀를 기울이고 있었던 모양이다. 달갑지 않은 화제 때문에 짐짓 외면해왔으나 이제 비로소 구미가 당기는 얘깃거리를 만났다는 식이었다. 탕 속의 노인네까지 참견할 눈치였다.

「동란 때 그만큼도 안 당한 사람이야 이 대한민국에 있겠소? 날 보시오. 사지육신이야 멀쩡하지. 비록 쭈그렁바가지가 되긴 했수다만…… 흉측한 상처 같은 거야 없지. 그거이 뭐 대단할 거 있소? 내 말은, 겉으로 뵈지 않는 상처가 더 크고 아푸다 그거지요.」

냉큼 말을 받은 쪽은 탕 속의 노인이었다. 시조 가락을 뽑던 그 걸걸한 목소리가 되묻고 있었다.

all over again. Towards the end of the war, his father was forcibly taken away from a street; and only three months and five days later, he was wounded. When he returned home that summer even before his wound healed, the wound was too severe and horrible to even look at. Now, however, as the ink of the letters written in history faded over time, the scar on his body looked shrunken, grimy, dried up, shriveled, like the dried end of a persimmon stalk.

He ran the scrubbing towel softly across the scar. Perhaps, that was when his father had become so fainthearted and timid towards the world. When his mother was still alive, her complaint about her husband was always about something like that, too: "That person came back home in body only. He left his soul behind on the battlefield. Day after day, he lies around in the room, glued to the floor. What on earth is he planning to do?"

In other words, her criticism was aimed at her husband's lack of goals or ambitions in the world. Was his father really that insincere towards life? In his memory, though, his father hadn't always been that way. Before they left their hometown and moved to the neighboring city of Daegu, he was

「그렇게 말하는 댁은 그래, 무슨 상처가 있다는 거요? 어디, 그 뵈지 않는 상처 얘기 한번 들어 봅시다.」

상대는 물론 사양하지 않았다.

「그거야 못 할 바 없지만서두, 말허자면 또 길지. 그럴 수밖에, 우리 같은 삼팔따라지들은 몸만 멀쩡했지 속이야 진작에 멍든 인생이니깐. 흉터가 문제겠소? 왼통 만신창이가 된 것을……」

얘기는 이제 그쪽으로 흘러갈 모양이었다. 빌미만 제공했을 뿐 금세 소외되어버린 두 부자는 어쩔 수 없이 가만히 귀 기울이고 있을 수밖에 도리가 없었다. 그에게 여전히 등을 내맡긴 노인네는 그나마 관심을 보였지만 그러나, 그로서는 도무지 그럴 기분이 내키지 않았다. 그는 두 개의 흉터를 번갈아 들여다보다가 목소리를 낮추어 다시 물었다.

「그럼 이쪽 상처는 어쩌다 생긴 거지요?」

노인의 대답은 건성이었다.

「머라꼬?」

「이쪽 흉터 말입니다. 이건 언제 생긴 거냐구요?」

「글씨 말이다. 그러니꺼네 거기…… 언제적 일이꼬? 깜깜하다 아이가. 도통 기억에 없다카이.」

enthusiastic about establishing his own businesses. Among most of his childhood memories of his father, opening a local newspaper branch office at the seat of a township office and suddenly knocking two rooms in one corner of the house into one in order to bring in a jersey knitting machine— these two remained intact in his memory. His father, at that time, must have been considered something of a visionary in his hometown of some 40 households. Otherwise, he couldn't have come up with such farfetched business ideas when everyone else, as usual, was just struggling in the dirt. Only a person of special abilities could have done it.

Then, he must have changed after he, empty-handed, relocated his entire family to Daegu. While living in the city, he must have lost all his goals and ambitions in the world, and become fainthearted and timid, and then finally degenerated into an incompetent man. Since the moving day, had he ever had any decent job? His father was so incompetent in urban life; and as much as he was incompetent, he was unlucky, too. That meant leaving the task of feeding mouths in the hands of the women in the family. His father had always been depending on

잠시 그를 돌아보는 듯하더니 금방 주의가 흩어졌다. 그리고는 화제에 끼어들었다.

「그라이꺼네 나이 서른둘에 삼팔선을 넘었구마는. 그것도 홀홀 단신이다 아입니꺼?」

나이가 지닌 친화력에 그는 새삼 놀라운 기분이 들었다. 노인에게서 떨어져 그는 사우나실로 들어갔다. 거기서도 고물인지 거물인지 몇 사람이 죽치고 앉아 땀을 뻘뻘 흘리고 있었다.

목욕탕에서 나왔을 때는 가등에 불이 들어와 있었다. 아파트의 창들도 드문드문 불이 켜졌다.

그는 집과는 반대 방향으로 길을 잡았다. 전화질도 그만두기로 하였다. 우선 비어 있는 속을 착실히 채우기로 하였다. 아주 좋은 기회다. 모처럼 아버지께 식사를 대접해드리기로 하자. 생각만으로도 기분이 좋아진 그는 상가가 밀집해 있는 거리로 진출하였다. 이른바 먹자골목에는 손님들이 한 패거리씩 꾀기 시작하는 시간이었다. 대여섯 개나 되는 돼지불고기집들은 너나 할 것 없이 식탁들을 죄다 길바닥으로 끌어내 놓았다. 말하자면 노천식당을 흉내 내고 있는 셈이다. 추운 겨울

the women: first, his first wife, then his older daughters, and now his second wife.

While he washed the lower parts of the old man's body, he found another scar. It was on the outer side of his right thigh. It was smaller than the one under the armpit, but to leave that much scar, it had most likely been a very serious injury in the first place. The white scar where the flesh had been torn was clearly visible even through the old man's heavily aged skin.

"When was it that you got injured here?" He scrubbed that area with his towel.

"Injured?"

The old man craned his neck to the left to look at the scar. "Where? Where's it?"

"Here, Father. It's quite a big one, isn't it?"

"Ah, you mean this one here?"

The old man felt for the scar with his fingers and said, "Isn't this the gunshot wound? You know, during the 6·25 War…"

"Really?" he asked him back, "That war wound is this one over here, isn't it?"

"Where?"

"Here."

He took the old man's hand and put it on the scar

이나 여름 장마철을 제외하고는 늘 그랬다. 저녁 무렵, 거기서 식구들과 둘러앉아 돼지갈비라도 뒤적거리고 있노라면 그런대로 기분이 괜찮았다. 그래도 이만큼은 하고 산다는 자부심 같은 게 스멀스멀 허파를 간지럽히는 것이었다. 비록 서민 아파트지만—서른 평 마흔 평짜리라면 더 말할 것 없고—서울을 지척에 둔 곳, 그것도 관악산과 청계산을 좌우에 거느린 천혜의 주거환경에다 그리고, 구질구질한 뒷골목이라고는 눈 씻고 봐도 없는, 1백 프로 계획도시인 이곳에 자리를 잡을 수 있었다는 사실에 대해 새삼 행복해지는 것이었다. 지난 4, 5년 동안 아파트 시세가 엄청나게 올랐다. 스물다섯 평짜리가 억대를 넘어선 지 오래라고 한다. 자칫했더라면 영영 기회를 놓칠 뻔하지 않았는가. 모두 억대부자가 되어버린 이 작은 도시의 주민들은 그래서 근년 들어 씀씀이도 더 푼푼해졌다. 주말이면 외식 나온 가족들로 하여 이 식당가가 으레 붐비곤 했던 것이다.

주문한 것이 그저 갈비 3인분과 소주 한 병에 지나지 않았는데도 그 두 가지 음식이 다 조금씩 남았다. 술이야 원래 그렇다 치고, 노인네의 식사량이 눈에 띄게 줄어 있었다. 먹성 한 가지는 타고난 양반인데, 라고 생각

146

near the armpit.

"This one's the gunshot wound. I can tell just by looking at it. It's from a piercing bullet wound, isn't it?" he continued.

"Is that right? You can tell?"

The old man's answer turned vague. It was a voice of someone who had just lost confidence. As if to rummage his memory, the old man's clumsy hand was feeling the scar uncertainly. Then, looking unconvinced, cocking his head to one side, he thought about it for a long while before he began to speak again. His voice still lacked confidence:

"Perhaps, you're right. Your real mother always said I could have lost all my ribs... If that darned fire-bean had been just a tiny bit more...whatever, I wouldn't be here today... It was beyond words, that horrible 6·25 War..."

"But you had it better than me."

Suddenly, someone broke in their conversation from the side of the bath. It was the old man that had been lying down on the floor. He seemed to have been listening to their conversation all along. He had deliberately looked away before because of the unwelcome subject, but now he looked quite interested in the new subject. Perhaps, this one

하자 그는 마음 한구석이 허전해져왔다.

「그래도 밥 묵능 거 하나는 끄떡없다 아이가.」

상에서 물러나 앉으며 노인이 말하였다. 「하루 삼세 끼, 꼬박꼬박 한 그릇씩 비워 낸다카이. 요새 젊은 앗들, 까딱하마 밥맛 없다카더라마는 내사 그기 무신 말인동 안죽 모르고 산다 아이가.」

「국수 좋아하셨잖아요. 한 근짜리는 혼자 자시곤 하셨는데……」

「하모! 그거 가주고는 한이 안 차더라. 근 반은 삶어야……」

「고기두요. 특히 기름 많은 걸 좋아하셨지요.」

「하모! 돼지비계 같은 거 좋더마는. 꾸시한 기…… 시장 바닥에서 와, 그거마 볶아 파는 데 안 있나. 돼지껍디 하고 말이다. 남들은 쪼매마 묵으도 설사한다카더라마는 어데, 내사 백날 가도 탈 한 분 안 나더라. 한창 묵을 때는 대접으로 수북하이 달락 해서 묵고 안 했나. 그래도 탈은 무신 탈. 끄떡없더라카이.」

결코 과장이 아님을 그는 잘 알고 있었다. 당신 말처럼 불과 한두 해 전만 해도 석이 녀석과 막상막하였는데 싶어 그는 또 마음이 허전해졌다. 갈비 3인분이라면

appealed to his appetite more. The old man in the hot-water tub seemed ready to get in on it, too.

"Is there anybody in this country who didn't suffer during the war? Look at me. I admit my body suffered no harm. Although it's shriveled like this...but there's no horrible scars on it. Even so, what's so great about it? I mean, the wounds you can't see from the outside are much bigger and more painful."

The old man in the tub quickly took up the man of invisible wounds. He asked in that husky voice crooning *sijo*, "Well then, what kind of wounds do you have? Let's hear it, the story of these invisible wounds."

His counterpart, of course, wasn't going to miss out on the chance.

"Since you've asked, I'll tell you, but it'll be a long story. Long, of course, are the life stories of us *sampal ttaraji* who crossed the 38th parallel to come to the South. Though unharmed on the outside, inside, we've already been done for long ago. Scars on the body are nothing in comparison. We're torn to pieces inside..."

Obviously, the story was going to continue spinning itself in that direction. The father and son,

녀석 혼자 해치울 양이었다.

그 다음으로 찾아간 곳은 안경가게였다. 노인의 고집을 막무가내로 꺾고 그는 기어이 새 안경을 맞추었다. 기왕이면 고급으로 해달랬더니, 이미 거래가 있어 낯이 익은 주인이 익살스럽게 대꾸하였다.

「고급이구 말구요. 이 정도면 국회의장급입니다.」

전혀 익살만은 아닐 터인데도 불구하고 노인의 얼굴에서 그것은 어쩐지 제값을 못 하는 것 같았다. 이마의 상처도 거슬리지만, 그보다 노인의 꾀죄죄한 입성 탓일 법하였다. 그는 옆의 쇼핑센터로 노인을 안내하였다. 지하 2층 지상 6층의 그 건물 안에는 모든 것이 다 있었다. 5층 남성복 매장에서 양복 한 벌을 골랐고, 3층에서 와이셔츠와 넥타이를, 그리고 2층 매장에서 쥐색의 중절모자를 찾아냈다. 구두는 굳이 바꿀 이유가 없었다. 그만큼 새것이었다. 처음에는 몇 번 사양하다가 결국은 그가 하자는 대로 수긋이 따라오던 노인네도 이 대목에 이르러서는 완강하였다.

「야가 와 이카노? 니 시방 누구한테 돈 자랑 하자카나 머 하노? 그 카든가 먼가는 안 갚어도 되능 기가?」

노인은 역정을 내기까지 하였다. 「니 한분 봐라 이거.

who had provided the momentum for the storytelling in the first place, were immediately ignored. So, willingly or unwillingly, they kept listening to the story in silence. His father, with his back still turned to him, showed some interest in the story, but he didn't feel like it at all. So, he looked into the two scars one after the other, and asked under his breath once more:

"Then how did you get this scar over here?"

The old man asked him back absentmindedly.

"What?"

"I mean the scar on this side. When did you get it?"

"Well, you see...let me think...when was it? I've no idea. I remember nothing, absolutely nothing, I'm telling you."

The old man was turning his head to look at him, but got immediately distracted and turned his attention back to the conversation between the other two old men.

"Let's see, I was thirty-two when I crossed the 38th parallel. All by myself at that."

He was yet again surprised to see the level of affinity one could have for anyone else who was about the same age. He walked away from his fa-

새거 아이가? 그동안 안 신고 나돗다가 인자 살마 얼매나 살꼬 싶어서 요새 들어 신는다카이. 내한테 새 구두가 머 하로 필요하겠노?」

그의 기분 같아서는 내친김에 머리끝에서부터 발끝까지 일습을 새로 갖춰드리고 싶었지만 더 이상 고집할 도리가 없었다. 대신에 문제의 혁대만은 기어이 바꾸어 매게 하였다. 마침내 쇼핑센터를 나섰을 때 노인의 모습은 완연히 달라져 있었다. 그는 헌옷 꾸러미를 한 손에 들고, 또 한 손으로는 노인의 팔을 부축한 채 가등이 하얗게 깔린 밤거리를 걸어갔다. 젊은 남녀 한 패거리가 와자지껄하며 지나갔다. 두 부자는 잠시 걸음을 멈추고 서 있었다.

아파트의 창문들은 이제 거의 다 환하게 불 켜진 상태였다. 승용차들이 하나씩 와닿고 있었다. 최근 몇 년 동안 차가 엄청나게 불어났다. 저녁 아홉 시만 지나면 더 이상 주차할 자리가 없다고 한다. 아내가 불평하던 말을 그는 문득 떠올렸다. 같은 계단을 쓰는 우리 10가구 중에 차가 없는 집은 딱 세 집뿐이라고 하였다. 그런데 정작 한심한 것은, 그 세 집이 다 훈장댁이라는 것이

ther and went in the sauna room. There, too, sat several "old things" or "bygone things" or whatever they called themselves, sweating profusely.

When they left the bathhouse, the streetlights were on. The windows of apartments were also lit here and there.

He chose the opposite direction to his apartment. He also decided to stop calling home. First of all, he wanted to stuff himself. This is the perfect chance. I'll treat Father to a meal, he thought.

Feeling happy just thinking about it, he proceeded to the shopping street. In the so-called eating-spree alley, it was time for the customers to arrive one party after another. Five or six eateries specializing in spiced-and-grilled pork had all of their tables taken out and set on the sidewalk. In their own way, they intended to imitate the open-air restaurants. Except for a hard winter or summer rainy season, the tables stayed outside. It felt quite good to sit around one of those tables with his family in the evening, flipping some pork ribs over the grill. On occasions like these, something like a sense of pride tickled his lungs flatteringly, confirming to him that he and his family were relatively

었다. 그는 혼자서 히죽이 웃었다. 낯선 이웃들이 서둘러 제 구멍을 찾아 기어들고 있었다. 그는 한 발 앞서 아파트의 계단을 성큼성큼 올라갔다. 아내의 귀가를 추호도 의심하지 않았다.

그를 맞아준 것은 그의 책가방이었다. 그 손때 묻은 물건이 철제 손잡이에 변함없이 걸려 있었다. 이번에야말로 아내의 귀가를 추호도 의심치 않았기 때문에 그는 조금 당황하였다. 아니, 좀 황당한 기분이 들었다. 이 여자가 어떻게 된 거지? 가출했나? 문득 그런 생각이 들었다. 그러나 그는 픽 웃고 말았다. 그리고 그 웃음이, 당황스럽고 황당하기까지 한 기분으로부터 그를 구해주었다. 가출? 그는 한 번 더 벌쭉 웃었다. 그런 충동을 느껴본 적은 있느냐고 물어보기는 해야지, 하고 그는 작정하였다. 집을 찾는 일을, 내가 자주 성가시게 느끼듯이 말이야.

「와 그라고 있노? 니 안사람, 안죽 안 왔나?」

뒤따라 올라온 노인이 더 놀라고 난감한 표정을 지었다. 「무신 일 생긴 거 아이가? 이래 기양 있어도 되는 기가? 어데 이부제라도 좀 물어보능 기 안 좋겠나 싶구마는……」

well off. Although living in the apartment complex built for the low-income bracket families, the residents there—especially those living in the 120- or 150-square-yard units—should have been happy about their advantageous living environment considering they lived not only very close to Seoul but also had Mt. Gwanak and Mt. Choenggye on either side of the complex. Furthermore, they were located in a 100-percent planned city, with absolutely no grubby back alleys. Over the previous four or five years, apartment prices had skyrocketed. It was said that the 100-square-yard units had long been sold at over one hundred million *won*. They could have missed the opportunity forever, couldn't they have? The residents in this small city, all of whom had become worth hundreds of millions, had been spending more generously for several years. Over the weekend, the eatery alley was always crowded with families dining out.

He ordered only three portions of ribs and a bottle of *soju*, and yet they had leftovers. His father had never been much of a drinker, but he noticed that his father ate considerably less than before. Father had been known as a man blessed with a large appetite, if nothing else. He felt an empty

「무슨 일 있을라구요. 괜한 걱정 마세요. 시내라도 나간 모양이지요 뭐.」

여기서 시내란 서울 쪽을 뜻한다. 그쪽으로 나들이해야 할 일인들 왜 없으랴. 그쪽은 1천만이 넘는 인구가 아글바글 모여 사느니만치 아내라고 하여 사고무친일 턱은 없다고 그는 생각하였다. 그 안엔 친구도 있고 일가붙이도 당연히 있으리라. 오랜만에 어울리다 본즉 늦어지고 있겠지. 애초부터 이럴 생각이야 아니었을 테지. 어쩌면 찻길이 막혔는지도 모른다. 아, 그놈의 서울 쪽 교통 사정이라니! 그는 열심히 궁리하면서 스스로 고개를 주억거리기도 하였다. 그런데 노인이 또 참견하였다.

「시상이 워낙 험해놔서…… 요새 젊은 여자들 밤길 댕기겠더나 어데.」

「걱정 마시라니깐요. 그렇게 젊은 여자도 아닙니다.」

그는 좀 짜증스럽게 대꾸한 다음 거의 충동적으로 옆집 초인종을 눌렀다. 그리고는 스스로도 놀라 뒤로 주춤 물러섰다. 다행히 반응이 없었다. 이 집도 비었는가 보다고 생각하고 등을 돌려세우는데 그때서야 여자의 조심스런 목소리가 흘러나왔다.

spot in his heart.

"When it comes to appetite though, I'm still going strong."

Drawing his seat back a little, the old man said. "A bowl of rice three times a day, like clockwork. Youngsters these days often complain about loss of appetite, but I've never, so far in my life, lacked appetite, you see."

"You liked noodles very much. You used to finish about half a kilo of noodles at a time..."

"Yes, of course! Actually, even that wasn't filling enough. I needed almost a kilo..."

"Meat, too. Especially fatty meat was your favorite."

"That's right! I loved to eat things like hog fat. The rich taste of broiled fat...! You remember the stalls in the outdoor market that sold only the stir-fried hog fat and skin, don't you? Other people complained that they got diarrhea after eating even a little bit of it. But, me? Never! I went there to eat hundreds of times but never had any trouble at all. At the peak of my eating, I used to ask for it heaped up in a soup bowl. Even that didn't give me any problems. I was A-OK."

He knew that there wasn't a hint of exaggeration

「누구세요?」

문은 닫힌 채였다. 아마도 렌즈 구멍으로 내다보고 있을 테지. 그는 상대가 이쪽을 잘 확인할 수 있도록 얼굴을 쳐들고 커다란 소리로 대꾸하였다.

「옆집인데요, 503홉니다만……」

「그래서요? 무슨 일이신데요?」

문이 열릴 기미는 없었다. 그는 잠시 주저하였다. 언젠가 아내에게 들은 바로는, 젊은 맞벌이 부부가 산다고 하였다. 목소리의 주인공은 아무래도 그 부인은 아닌 듯 나이와 촌스러움이 느껴졌다. 나이 든 가정부이거나 또는 시골서 올라온 노모인 모양이라고 짐작되었다. 별 기대 없이 그는 물었다.

「혹시 우리 집사람 어디 간다는 얘기 없었습니까?」

「글쎄요, 암말 없었구만요. 안에 안 계시우?」

「네, 어딜 갔는지 없구만요. 실례 많았습니다, 감사합니다.」

그는 닫힌 문에다 대고 두어 번 머리를 숙였다. 저쪽에서는 더 이상 대꾸가 없었다. 하지만 이쪽의 거동을 계속 지켜보고 있는 듯 은밀한 기척이 느껴졌다.

두 부자는 다시 아파트 계단을 내려왔다. 더 이상 갈

in his father's recollections. As his father said, as late as the previous year or the one before, his father was eating as much as Sok-i. He felt hollow inside once more. Sok-i would have finished the three portions of grilled ribs all by himself.

After the meal, they went to an optician's. Having beaten his father in a fierce war of obstinacy, he was able to get his father a new pair of glasses in the end. When he told the shop owner he might as well get the old man a quality frame, the owner, who recognized him as one of his customers, gave a witty answer.

"This is a quality frame, indeed. It's good even for the Speaker of the National Assembly."

The optician's answer couldn't have been all wit, but the spectacles didn't seem to show their quality all that well on the old man's face. The scratch on the forehead could be partly to blame, but the old man's shabby clothes seemed to be the real culprit. He showed the old man to a shopping center nearby. It was a six-story building with an additional two stories underground. It had everything one needed in it. They bought a suit in the men's wear section on the fifth floor, a shirt and a necktie on the third floor, and a dark-grey soft hat on the

곳이 마땅치 않았다. 단지 안길을 조금 걷다가 필경엔 어린이 놀이터로 되돌아왔다. 아까 그 벤치에 누가 먼저랄 것도 없이 자리들을 잡았다.

놀이터는 텅 비어 있었다. 그네도, 미끄럼틀도, 시소도 한결같이 허전한 모습이었다. 철봉대며 회전그네며 정글 같은 철근 구조물들이 가등 아래 차갑게 보였다. 모래 바닥에는 아이들이 남긴 무수한 발자국들이 무슨 상형문자이기나 하듯이 가득 펼쳐져 있었다. 과자 포장지들이 여기저기 굴러다니고, 그리고 세발자전거 한 대가, 아마도 윗도리일 법 싶은 옷가지 한 점과 함께 가쪽에 버려져 있었다.

「저거 보래이.」노인이 그쪽으로 눈을 주며 입을 뗐다.

「자전거고 머고 말캉 냇삐리고 갔대이. 요새 앗들, 머 하나 기릅은 기 없다카이.」

그는 잠자코 듣기만 하였다.

「핵교 댕기는 앗들도 똑같닥 하더마는. 머든지 살 줄만 알지 지 물건 간수하는 거는 도통 관심 밖이라카이. 너거 때하고는 마이 다르다 아이가.」

그는 잠자코 웃기만 하였다. 대구에서 다니던 초등학교 시절, 어쩌다 필통을 통째로 잃어 먹고는 엉엉 울었

second floor. There was no need to get a new pair of shoes. The old man's were quite new. At first, the old man had declined several times to get anything for himself, but in the end, he relented and let his son buy him things. However, when it came to purchasing a new pair of shoes, he simply wouldn't give in.

"What's the matter with you? Are you trying to make a show of your money, or what? Don't you need to pay off that card or something?"

The old man yelled out at last in a fit of temper. "Just look at my shoes yourself, here. Aren't these new? I used to keep this pair stashed away, but recently I began wearing them because I know that my days are numbered. Why would I need new shoes?"

If he was allowed to do as he pleased, he wanted to get the old man an entire set of new things from top to toe, but there was no way he could insist any longer. In the end, though, he at least succeeded in making the old man change the belt in question. By the time they left the shopping center, the old man's appearance had completely changed. He held a bundle of the old clothes in one hand and with the other, held the old man by the arm.

던 기억이 떠올라 웃음을 더 깊게 하였다. 노인은 말을 좀 더 계속할 듯하더니 그만두었다. 새삼스럽게 주위를 한 차례 두리번거렸다. 그리고는 앉은키를 낮추어 윗몸을 등받이에다 기대었다. 쥐색 중절모 아래에서 국회의장급 안경이 가등 빛을 받아 번쩍거렸다. 그렇게 한동안 허공에다 무연히 눈길을 주고 있다가 노인이 불쑥 말하였다.

「그느마를 우야마 좋겠노?」

피곤과 졸음기가 묻어 있는 목소리였다. 그는 번쩍 정신이 들었다.

「예? 누구요?」

대답이 없더니 한참 만에 노인은 또 중얼댔다. 「차말로 그느마를 우야마 좋겠노?」

그리고는 한숨을 후우 하고 내쉬었다. 그는 두 번 다시 묻지 않았다. 저쪽 아이들 중에 어느 녀석이 또 당신속 썩일 짓을 저질렀나보다고 생각했을 뿐이었다. 그 동생들을 두고 생각하노라면 그로서는, 배가 다르다기보다 세대가 다르다는 느낌이 더 앞서곤 하였다. 하긴 그들과 최소한 20년 이상의 틈이 가로놓여 있지 않는가. 세대가 다른 만큼 의식이나 정서가 다르고, 그런 것

And they walked side by side along the night street illuminated white by the street lamps. A group of young men and women passed by clamorously. The father and son stopped walking and stood there for a while.

By then, almost all of the apartment windows were brightly lit. Cars started to arrive one after another at the complex. Over several years, the number of cars had increased dramatically. It was said that there was no more parking spaces available after nine in the evening. He was suddenly reminded of his wife's complaint. According to her, there were only three households, among the ten sharing the same stairs in their apartment building, that didn't own a car. Truly pathetic was the fact that all three of them were teacher's families. He grinned to himself. His neighbors, unfamiliar though to him, were coming back to their own holes in haste. He climbed up the stairs briskly ahead of them. He had no doubt at all that his wife was already back at home.

However, what received him was his bag. That hand-stained bag was still hanging on the metal doorknob. He was slightly taken aback since he

이 다른 만큼 당연히 생활 양태가 달랐던 것이다.

「너거들하고는 우째 그래 다르꼬……」

노인은 또 한 차례 싶은 한숨을 토해놓았다. 입을 다
물고만 있을 수가 없어 그는 다시 입을 열었다.

「말씀해 보세요. 무슨 일이 있는 거군요?」

그러나 노인의 대꾸는 정작 가벼웠다.

「아이다. 일은 무신 일, 기양 쪼매 속상한 기 있어 그
카는 기지 머……」

그 쪼매 속상한 것이 뭐냐고 그는 묻지 않았다. 캐묻
는다고 해서 대답할 노인네도 아니라는 사실을 그는 잘
알고 있는 터였다. 서로를 위해 어떤 선은 필요하다고
그도 수긍하는 바였다. 더 이상 헤쳐놓는 일은 두 쪽을
다 성가시고 피곤하게 만들 것이었다. 대화가 끊긴 채
두 부자는 조용히 앉아 있었다. 하루의 피곤이, 이제야
말로 더 이상 감당해내기 어려운 무게로 짙게 느껴져왔
다. 두 사람은 어느새 꾸벅꾸벅 졸기 시작하였다.

그는 밤길을 가고 있었다. 숲이 무성한 산길이었다.
달은 있었는지 없었는지 모르겠다. 길은 어둡고 험하고
그리고, 너무 멀고 멀었다. 산 두 개를 넘어야 이모 집이
었다. 아버지는 늘 그를 데리고 나섰다. 비록 열 살 남짓

hadn't even dreamed of not finding his wife back at home at this hour of the evening. Come to think of it, the situation seemed outright absurd. What was the matter with this woman? Had she run away from home? The thought briefly crossed his mind. But then he ended up laughing to himself. And that laugh waved away his confused and absurd thoughts. Run away? he gave another silent laugh, opening his mouth wider this time.

"I'll at least ask her if she's ever been tempted to do so," he thought, "Just like me. I often find homecoming troublesome."

"What's the matter? Your wife hasn't come back yet?"

The old man, who finally caught up with him, looked more surprised and perplexed than he was. "Perhaps, something's happened to her? Is it okay if we just keep waiting? I think we should ask your neighbors..."

"Nothing's happened to her, Father. Not to worry. She's probably gone to the City or something."

By "the City," he meant Seoul. 'Why wouldn't she have an occasion to visit Seoul?' In the city swarming with ten million people, it was not likely that she had no one to visit. 'She probably had friends

한 때였지만 그래도 밤중 산길에서는 마음 든든한 짝이 된다는 것이었다. 그 무렵 아버지는 자주 이모댁을 찾곤 했었다. 그의 가족이 고향을 떠나 대구 바닥으로 나앉은 직후였고 몹시 궁하게 살 때였으므로 방문의 이유는 자명하였다. 차편이라고는 단지 그것밖에 없었다. 벽촌 간이역인 남성현역에는 자정이 넘어서야 닿았다. 거기서부터 큰 산봉우리 둘을 걸어서 넘어야 했던 것이다. 이모댁에 닿고 보면 온몸이 땀으로 흠씬 젖어 있곤 하였다. 어린 그에게는 힘겨운 길이기도 했지만, 그러나 무엇보다 무서움 때문이었다. 인가도 없는 험한 산길을 오밤중에 넘는 일은 늘 오금을 저리게 했던 것이다. 무섬기를 쫓기 위해 아버지는 자꾸 말을 시켰다. 때로는 노래를 부르게도 하였다. 그가 굳이 입을 다물고 있을라치면 당신이 대신하였다. 어린 그를 상대로 온갖 얘기들 을 늘어놓곤 했던 것이다. 이제는 거의 아무것도 기억해낼 수가 없다. 그러나 잊혀지지 않는 말도 있다. 언제던가, 당신이 불쑥 꺼냈던 수수께끼가 그것이었다.

「시상에서 젤로 무섭은 기 먼지 아나?」

그는 열심히 궁리한 끝에 답변했었다.「호랑이요.」

and relatives living there. She may have been with some of them now. Someone she hadn't seen for a long time, unaware of the passage of time. Not that she'd planned ahead to return home late. Or, she was stuck in traffic. How terrible the traffic jam in Seoul could be!' He kept mulling over the possibilities, nodding his head every now and then. Then, the old man cut in on his thoughts again.

"It's such a dangerous world...young women these days, it's not safe for them to be out at night, is it?"

"I'm telling you, Father. Don't worry. Besides, she's not that young anymore."

He answered a bit irritated, and, almost impulsively, pressed the bell button on the door of the apartment next to his. Then, he reeled back, surprised at his own action. Fortunately, there was no response. Thinking no one was in that apartment, either, he was turning around when he heard the wary voice of a woman from inside.

"Who is it?"

The door stayed closed. She was probably looking out through the lens hole. He answered in a loud voice, his face raised in order to help the woman check him out.

「호랑이가 머가 무섭노.」

아버지는 단호히 고개를 내저었다. 「호랑이라카는 짐 승은 영물이라 함부로 사람을 해꼬지 하는 일이 없다 아이가. 지 배 부르마 퇴끼 새끼 한 마리 손 안 댄다카 이.」

「그라마 구신요 구신, 도깨비 같은……」

「차말로 구신 낮밥 묵는 소리 하네. 시상에 구신이 어 딨고 도깨비가 어딨더노? 그런 거를 미신이라 안 카나. 핵교 댕기는 아가 우예 그런 소리를 하노?」

「아부지는요? 그라마 아부지는 머가 젤로 무섭어예?」

「사람 아이가. 세상에서 젤로 무섭은 기 바로 사람인 기라. 이런 데서 생판 낯선 사람하고 턱 마주쳐봐라. 얼 매나 간이 오구라붙을 일이겠노. 차라리 호랭이가 낫 지. 도깨비고 구신이 어데 따로 있나. 인간이 바로 그기 라카이.」

그는 물론 이해할 수 없었고, 그래서 아무런 대꾸도 하지 못했었다. 유독 이때의 얘기만 지금까지 잊혀지지 않고 머릿속에 남아 있는 까닭이 무엇일까 하고 그는 곰곰 생각에 잠겼다. 무엇일까…… 무엇일까…… 까닭 은…… 그러던 어느 순간에 그는 흠칫 놀라 고개를 쳐

"I live next door, Number 503..."

"So? What's this about?"

There was no sign of the woman opening the door. He hesitated for a moment. He remembered his wife saying that a young couple lived in that apartment. The voice didn't sound young; it was rather old and rural-sounding, not at all a young woman's. He assumed that it was the young woman's mother from the country or an elderly housemaid. Not expecting much, he asked:

"I wonder if you heard from my wife that she was going out somewhere?"

"No, I didn't hear anything. Isn't she in?"

"No, she's not. I'm just wondering where she's gone. I'm sorry to have bothered you. Thank you."

He bowed a couple of times to the closed door. There was no more answer from the woman. Nevertheless, he could feel that she was still watching him secretly from behind the door.

The father and son climbed back down the stairs. He couldn't think of any more places to go. They strolled around in the complex for a while and eventually came back to the playground. They sat down on the same bench, neither of them inquiring of the other.

들었다.

깜박 졸았던 모양이다. 턱 언저리에 무언가 스멀거리는 느낌이 어서 손등으로 훔치고 본즉 침이었다. 그는 삐딱하게 흘러내린 안경을 고쳐 쓴 다음 주위를 뚤레뚤레 둘러보았다. 텅 빈 놀이터, 어두운 하늘, 가지런히 불켜진 창들 따위가 몽롱한 시선에 잡혀들었다. 바로 옆자리에서 잠이 든 노인의 모습을 발견한 것은 되레 나중의 일이었다. 어쨌거나, 노인은 머리를 가슴팍에다 잔뜩 꺾은 채 잠이 들어 있었다. 예의 쥐색 중절모는 땅바닥에 굴러떨어진 지 아마도 오래인 듯 민둥한 정수리를 그대로 드러낸 채였다.

노인이 느닷없이 고개를 불쑥 쳐들더니 뭐라고 외쳐댔다. 두 손을 내저으며 무언가를 내쫓는 시늉까지 하였다. 꿈을 꾸고 있는가보다고 그는 생각하였다. 가위눌린 사람의 몸짓이었다.

「왜 그러세요? 아버지. 아버지!」

그는 노인을 흔들어 깨웠다. 그러자 노인은 냅다 비명을 지르며 그를 거칠게 떼밀어냈다. 칠순 노인의 힘이라고는 믿어지지 않을 만큼 세찬 것이어서 자칫 뒤로 벌렁 나가떨어질 뻔하였다. 그는 망연자실한 채 멀거니

The playground was deserted. The swings, slides, seesaws—they all looked lonesome. The iron structures, like the horizontal bars, gyro-swings, and jungle gym—all looked cold in the light of the street lamps. In the sandbox, countless children's footprints were scattered all over, as if they were some kind of hieroglyphics. Cookie wrappers were lying here and there; and on one side, outside the sandbox, there was a tricycle, abandoned along with an item of clothing, probably a jacket.

"Look at that." The old man broke the silence, turning to look at him.

"Look what they've left behind, the tricycle and whatnot. Kids these days, they don't make much of anything."

He listened in silence.

"They say even the school kids are like that now. They only want to buy things, but never even think about taking care of them. They're quite different from kids when you were small, aren't they?"

He just smiled and didn't say anything. He remembered the time when he, as an elementary school kid living in Daegu, lost his pencil case and had wailed himself hoarse. His smile broadened. The old man was about to say some more, but

지켜보고 있을 수밖에 다른 도리가 없었다. 그는 묵묵히 허리를 굽혀 발치께에 나뒹굴고 있는 모자를 집어 들었다. 왠지 손이 후들후들 떨렸다.

노인은 잠시 의식을 챙기는 듯싶었다. 들숨날숨을 한 차례씩 길고 요란스럽게 하고는 내처 빈 입을 쩝쩝 다시고 나더니 비로소 부스스 얼굴을 쳐들었던 것이다. 안경이 코끝에 걸려 있었다.

「가마이 보자…… 여가 어데고?」

잠긴 목소리였다. 장거리 전화를 통해 듣던 바로 그 음성이었다.

「내가 깜북 했던갑제?」

「저두요……」

그는 웃으며 대꾸하였다.「당연하시죠 뭐. 먼 길 오셨겠다, 목욕하셨겠다, 그리고 또, 막 식사하셨지요.」

「하모, 그라고 보이까네 쪼매 곤하구마는…… 늙으마 잠이 없닥 하는 거도 다 빈말 같더라. 내사 아무데서나 꿉벅꿉벅 잘 존다카이.」

「무슨 꿈 꾸셨어요? 뭐라고 소리치시던데요?」

「개가, 껌둥 강새이가 항꾼에 시 마리나 나타나가주고 나한테 막 안 덤비나. 어찌나 씩껍 묵었는지 등때기

stopped short. He suddenly looked around the place. Then he leaned against the back of the bench, arching his back a little. Under the visor of the soft hat, his Speaker-of-the-National-Assembly spectacles glistened in the street-lamp light. After staring into space for a while, the old man, out of the blue, blurted out:

"What am I supposed to do with that child?"

The old man's voice sounded muffled in fatigue and drowsiness. He was startled to attention.

"Pardon me, Father? Who do you mean?"

After a long silence, the old man muttered:

"Really, what am I to do with the child?"

Then, the old man let out a long sigh. He didn't repeat his question. He just assumed that one of the children over in Daegu had done something wrong, and it was that that had been troubling the old man. Between he and his younger siblings on his stepmother's side, he always felt a gap more in terms of belonging to different generations than in having different mothers. In fact, there was an over twenty-year age difference. The generation gap led to an emotional gap, which, in turn, led to the inevitable difference in life-style.

"Why on earth are they so different from you

가 다 척척하다카이.」

노인은 그러면서 등 쪽으로 손을 가져갔다. 「요새 꿈자리가 좀 시끄럽다 아이가. 눈만 붙였닥 하마 벨 꿈을 다 꾼대이.」

「자리가 불편해서 그러겠지요 뭐.」

그는 우정 대수롭지 않게 받아들이고는 일어났다.

아무도 전화를 받지 않았다. 공중전화 부스에서 나온 그는 아파트로 갔다. 계단을 오르면서, 이게 몇 번째인가 셈해보았지만 자꾸 헷갈리기만 하여 그만두었다. 5층까지 올라갔을 때 변함없이 그를 맞아준 것은 자신의 손때 묻은 가방뿐이었다. 이런 상황을 진작부터 예측해왔던 것처럼, 또는 기왕에 잘 길들여지기라도 한 것처럼 그는 담담하였다. 돌아서 층계를 다시 되짚어 내려오다가 석이 녀석을 떠올리고는 한마디 투덜댔다. 그녀석이 제 집구석을 기억하고는 있는 건가?

놀이터로 되돌아와보니 노인은 다시 잠들어 있었다. 이번에는 벤치 위에 모잽이로 드러누운 채였다. 옹색한 자리라 잔뜩 움츠린 자세여서 노인의 몸뚱이가 더 작고 잔약하게 느껴졌다. 머리맡에 모자와 안경이 얌전하게 놓여 있었다. 그는 그것을 집어 들고는 그 자리에 앉았

children..."

The old man breathed another long-drawn sigh. He couldn't just stay silent anymore, so he asked him again:

"Please, tell me, Father. Something's happened, hasn't it?"

However, the old man answered unexpectedly light-heartedly. "No. Nothing's happened. It's just I'm a little bit worried about something, nothing really serious..."

He didn't ask what that little worry of his was about. He knew only too well that the old man would never tell him, no matter how hard he pressed. He agreed that a certain line needed to be drawn in order to keep peace between them. Inquiring any further would only make both of them harassed and tired. When their conversation was over, they just continued sitting there in silence. The fatigue from the long day finally began pressing down on them, heavily and beyond resistance. Before long, the two were nodding off.

He was walking in the dark of night, He was following a trail in a densely wooded mountain. He wasn't sure if the moon was out or not. The trail was dark and rugged, and they still had a long, long

다. 고개를 젖히고 밤하늘을 쳐다보았다. 하현달이 떠올라 있었다. 오늘이 며칠이던가? 잠시 더듬어보았지만 얼른 생각나지 않았다. 다시 고개를 꺾고 노인을 내려다보았다. 깊은 잠에 떨어진 듯싶었다. 멀고 먼 길을 훌쩍 떠나버린 것처럼 몹시 적막한 느낌이었다. 그래서일까, 아버지와 동무하여 밤의 산길을 걷던 때가 불쑥 떠올랐다. 그러나 그 회상은 금방 차단되었다. 갑자기 앙칼진 여자의 비명 소리가 터져나왔기 때문이었다. 그는 고개를 쳐들 고 주위를 둘러보았다. 불 켜진 창마다 똑같은 소리들이 쏟아져 나오고 있었다. 목하 인기 절정의 텔레비전 연속극이 방영 중인 모양이었다.

『문 앞에서』, 도서출판 세계사, 1997

way to go. His aunt's house was two mountains away. His father always took him along. He was just over ten, but his father said even a young boy like him would be a reliable partner while traveling through the mountains at night.

At the time, his father often visited his aunt's. It was right after his family left their hometown and moved to Daegu, only to struggle in poverty, which made the reason for their frequent trips to his aunt's self-evident. There was only one way of transportation. The train arrived at Namseong Prefecture station, an outback, provisional train station, after midnight. From there, they had to walk over two big mountains. By the time they got to his aunt's, they were soaking wet in their own sweat.

To a small boy like him, it was an overly difficult trip, but what really made it truly arduous was his fear. Walking along the deserted mountain trails at midnight made him shrink inside himself. To relieve him from fear, his father kept talking to him. Sometimes, his father even asked him to sing loudly. If he stayed silent, his father would sing a song himself. To him, a mere child, his father would ramble on and on about all kinds of things. He remembered almost nothing of what his father had talked about at the time. Nevertheless, there was one thing he had never forgotten. One night, his father suddenly gave him a riddle to solve:

"What's the scariest thing in the world?"

He thought hard about it and answered: "A tiger."

"Why! A tiger's not scary at all."

His father shook his head slowly. "Tigers are sacred animals and they never harm humans rashly, you see. When they're full, they wouldn't touch even a rabbit."

"Then, ghosts, like goblins..."

"My goodness! You're really talking nonsense now. There're no such things as ghosts or goblins in the world. That's called superstition. How can a school kid like yourself believe in such things?"

"What about you, Father? What scares you the most?"

"Why! It's humans. People are the scariest things in the world. Just imagine meeting a stranger in a place like this. How scared stiff you'd be. Meeting a tiger would be much better than that. Ghosts and goblins aren't separate from humans. In fact, humans are ghosts and goblins themselves."

As a child, of course, he couldn't understand what his father was talking about, so he couldn't say anything in response. Why then, he wondered, did this particular conversation still remain in his memory while all the others had gone? What... what... What's the reason? ... At some moment, he suddenly raised his head startled.

He must have dozed off. Feeling something creeping down his chin, he wiped it with the back of his hand and saw that it was his saliva. He readjusted his glasses that had slipped down and hung crookedly on his nose; and he looked around the place several times. A deserted playground, a dark sky, rows of lit windows, and so forth came into his blurred vision. Only later did he find the old man sleeping right beside him. The old man was asleep with his head buried deep in his chest. The bald crown of his head was exposed, his grey soft hat fallen to the ground, perhaps for a while now.

The old man abruptly threw his head back and yelled something. He waved both of his hands in the air, as if he were chasing something away. He thought the old man was dreaming. It was a gesture of a person having a nightmare.

"What is it, Father? Father!"

He shook the old man to wake him. Then the old man suddenly pushed him away violently, screaming piercingly. The old man was unbelievably strong for a 70-year-old man and he almost fell over backward. He had no choice but to watch the old man, dumbfounded. He reached down and picked up the hat lying near his feet. For no reason, his hands were trembling badly.

The old man seemed to try to come to his senses for a while. Taking a long, noisy breath in and then out, the old man smacked his lips a couple of times, finally lifting his face slowly. His glasses were hanging on the tip of his nose.

"Let's see...where am I?"

His father spoke in a hoarse voice. It was the same voice that he'd heard over the long-distance call.

"I dozed off, didn't I?"

"So did I, Father..."

He laughed. "It's only natural you should feel beat. You've traveled far, taken a hot bath, and then just had dinner too."

"You're right. Come to think of it, I'm a little bit tired... They say one sleeps less with age, but if you ask me, it's just nonsense. I doze off anytime, anywhere."

"Did you have any dreams? You were yelling in

your sleep."

"Dogs. Black dogs. Three in all, showed up and pounced on me. They scared the hell out of me. Look, my back is still sweaty."

The old man brought his hand to his back. "Lately, I keep having unsettling dreams. Whenever I fall asleep, I have all kinds of strange dreams."

"Maybe, it's because your bed isn't comfortable."

He tried to be nonchalant and raised himself from the bench.

No one answered the phone. Leaving the phone booth, he was headed for his apartment. He climbed up the stairs and tried to count how many times he had walked up the stairs that day, but he kept getting confused and gave it up. On the fifth floor, it was once again his hand-stained bag waiting for him. As if he had already expected for it to happen, or as if he had been well trained for it, he felt calm. He turned around; and tracing his way back down the stairs, he remembered his son, Sok-i and muttered to himself: "Does the boy even remember his home?"

When he returned to the playground, the old man had fallen asleep again. This time, he was lying on his side on a bench. Lying in the fetal position, the old man looked smaller and even more fragile. Near the old man's head, the hat and glasses were laid neatly side by side. He picked them up and sat down. He leaned his head back and looked up at the night sky. A waning moon was up there. What was the date today? He tried to think, but the answer didn't come to mind readily. He looked down at the old man. He seemed fast asleep. He felt so lonely, as if he had just started on a long, long journey without any promise of return. Perhaps that was why he was reminded again of the night trips he and his father had made together through the mountains. The recollection, however, was quickly interrupted. Suddenly, the ear-piercing scream of a woman burst the night calm. He raised his head and looked around. From each lit window, the same sound was pouring out. It seemed that a TV soap opera, which was enjoying the highest ratings at the moment, was on.

Translated by Jeon Miseli

해설

Afterword

아버지와 아들, 그들만의 아름다운 저녁

김한식 (문학평론가)

시작은 이렇다. 휴대전화가 보급되기 전인 1990년대 초반, 서울 근교에 살고 있지만 남쪽 먼 곳에 직장을 두고 주말부부로 살아가는 사십대 후반의 남자는 문이 잠긴 아파트 문 앞에서 서성거린다. 그는 한 달에 몇 번 집에 오지만 오늘따라 연락 없이 올라와 빈집에 들어가지 못하고 있다. 한참을 서성거린 후 그는 자기 외의 다른 사람이 집 근처에서 서성거리는 것을 발견하게 된다. 다른 남자는 고향 대구에서 연락 없이 아들의 집을 찾아온 그의 아버지였다. 잠긴 문 안으로 들어가지 못한 두 '가장'은 문 밖에서 우연히 하루 저녁을 함께 보내게 된다. 이 소설은 묘한 상황에 만나 저녁 시간을 함께 보

Father and Son,
a Beautiful Evening All to Themselves

Kim Han-sik (literary critic)

Lee Dong-ha's novella begins with a man in his late forties standing outside the locked door to his apartment in the outskirts of a nearly cellphone-less, 1990s Seoul. The man has a job far away from home in the southern part of Korea and returns home only once a month. When he arrives home one day without informing his family of his home-coming, he realizes that he cannot get in his apart-ment since no one is home to open the door for him. After a long while, he happens to find another person waiting outside the door to his apartment. It is his father who has come to Seoul from his hometown Daegu to visit him, also unannounced.

내는 부자(父子)의 이야기이다.

일반적으로 우리 사회에서 중년을 넘어선 부자가 단둘이 긴 시간을 함께 보낼 일이 많지는 않다. 여러 이유로 한국에서 부자관계는 다정하고 다감한 관계라기보다 점잖고 어색한 관계인 경우가 많다. 지금은 달라졌다고 하지만 아버지는 침범할 수 없는 권위를 가지고 있었으며, 다른 가족구성원과는 떨어져 홀로 존재하는 섬과 같은 존재였다. 쉽게 감정을 드러내지 않고 가정 내에서보다는 가정 밖에서 자기를 드러내야 하는 사람이었다.

이 소설의 아버지들 역시 가족이지만 조금은 가족 밖에서 살아가는 인물들이다. 아들의 경우 천 리나 떨어져 있는 직장에서 외롭게 지내다 주말에야 겨우 집으로 돌아오곤 한다. 교육문제나 주거환경 때문에 가족들은 여전히 서울 근교에 남겨둘 수밖에 없다. 경제적인 문제가 아니면 가족들이 평소에 그를 긴히 찾지도 않는다. 경제적 능력마저 변변치 못한 그의 아버지는 더 말할 것도 없다. 아버지는 새로 결혼한 아내와 통제하기 어려운 아들과 함께 살면서 문제가 생기면 반항의 뜻으로 전처 아들을 찾아 상경하는 일을 반복한다. 자신에

Thus, the two "heads of family" come to spend that evening together outside by accident. In a nutshell, *Outside the Door* is a story of a father and son caught in an odd situation and compelled to spend an evening together after their chance meeting.

Generally speaking, in our society, a father and his son, both past their middle years, are not likely to spend a long time together just by themselves. For various reasons, the father-son relationship in Korea tends to be more courteous and awkward than familiar and emotional. There have been visible changes in the family relations in Korea; nevertheless, a father still retains an inviolable authority, the patriarch, and as such, retains an existence of his own separated from the rest of his family, a lone island of familial relations. He is not supposed to reveal his emotions easily and is expected to prove himself outside rather than inside his own home.

The father and son in this fiction, each of whom has his own family, also live a bit as outsiders in their respective homes. The son barely comes back home once a month, leading a lonely life for the majority of the year at a job 250 miles away from home. For the sake of his children's education and

게 다른 아들이 있다는 점을 아내에게 보여주기 위한 '치사한' 시위이다. 그들은 가정은 밖에서 얻은 피로와 스트레스를 풀고 삶의 의욕과 활력을 재충전받는 공간이라는 말을 실감하지 못한다. 오히려 자신들은 늘 잠긴 문 밖에서 서성거리고 있었다고 생각한다.

그렇다고 이 소설이 가정에서 소외당한 가장들의 문제를 주제로 삼고 있는 것은 아니다. 가족의 갈등이나 화해를 인상적인 사건을 통해 본격적으로 다루고 있다고 보기도 어렵다. 그가 늦도록 돌아오지 않는 가족을 원망하기도 하지만 작가는 그것을 심각한 수준으로 발전시키지는 않는다. 가족들에게도 일상이 있고 지금의 늦은 귀가도 그 일상에서 크게 벗어나지 않으리라는 사실을 그는 순순히 받아들인다. 이 소설의 중심 서사와 주제는 우연한 만남을 통해 아들이 아버지의 삶을 이해해가는 과정에 있다. 문 안이 아닌 문 밖에서 본 아버지의 모습을 통해 아들은 아버지가 살았던 시대, 그가 만났던 사람 그리고 그의 고민까지 이해하게 된다. 마음 속에 남아 있던 아버지에 대한 의문이나 서운한 감정도 녹아내린다.

집에 들어갈 수 없는 아들은 안경점, 양복점, 식당, 목

a better residential environment, he has no choice but to settle his family in an apartment on the outskirts of Seoul. His wife and children do not need him around unless they have money problems. The situation is worse for his father who is not even a reliable breadwinner. Whenever the old man is in conflict with his second wife or intractable teenage son, he, in a gesture of protest, makes a trip to Seoul where the family of his eldest son by his former wife lives. It is a "base" action of protest made to show his present wife that he has another son to turn to. Neither the son nor the father agrees that "home is a space where one gets relieved of the fatigue and stress from the outside world and recharged with a fresh supply of vital energy." Rather, they feel as if they have always been standing around outside the entrances of their own homes.

Nonetheless, this fiction does not deal with the issue of alienated fathers as its main theme. Nor does it scrutinize familial conflicts and seek resolutions through some impressive series of events. The son resents his wife who does not return home until late in the evening, and yet, the motif of resentment is not developed to a serious degree, either. The son meekly accepts the facts that his

욕탕으로 아버지를 모시고 다닌다. 새삼스럽게 추레한 아버지의 모습이 마음에 걸렸기 때문이다. 함께 목욕을 하면서 그는 아버지의 겨드랑이 아래쪽에 길쭉하게 드러나 있는 흉터를 발견한다. 전쟁통에 생긴 상처이다. 그는 전쟁의 상처가 단순히 아버지의 신체뿐 아니라 정신에도 영향을 미쳤으리라 생각한다. 아버지는 세상에서 제일 무서운 게 사람이라고 주저 없이 말하는 분이다. 그만큼 그가 살아온 세월은 험했고 개인이 견디기에는 벅찬 것이었다.

젊은 시절 그는 아버지에게 불만이 많았다. 평생을 가난 속에서 살았고 유난히 무능력했으며 그런 만큼 매사에 불운한 분이라 여겼다. 그런 그가 새삼스럽게 아버지를 이해하게 된 것은 그가 어느새 아버지의 모습을 닮아버렸기 때문인지도 모른다. 예상치 않은 시간과 장소에서 아버지를 보았을 때 그는 자기 코앞에서 맞바라보고 있는 좀 더 늙고 좀 더 초췌해 보이는 자기를 보았던 것이다. 구체적인 삶의 과정이 다르기는 했지만 가장으로서 한 가정을 짊어지고 견디어온 세월의 무게는 온전히 그들의 얼굴에 남아 있었고, 그것도 아버지와 너무도 닮은 모습을 띠고 있었던 셈이다.

family have their own everyday life and that their late homecoming does not transgress far beyond the boundaries of their everyday routines. At the narrative and thematic core of this novel is the process in which the son comes to understand his father's life via an opportunity provided by their unexpected meeting. Meeting his father outside the door, rather than inside, the son is at last able to see his father from a different perspective. The son eventually understands the turbulent times his father has lived in, the kinds of people he has met, and the nature of the agony he has suffered. The suspicion and resentment the son used to harbor against his father dissolve at the same time.

The son, unable to enter his apartment, takes his father to one place after another: a public bath, an optometrist's office, a men's clothing store, and a restaurant. The man's father's shabby appearance weighs on his mind. While taking a bath together, the son finds a long scar under his father's armpit. The scar was left by a bullet wound his father suffered during the war. The son thinks that the war wound has affected not only his father's body but his spirit as well. His father, without any hesitation at all, tells his ten-year-old son that the scariest

이 소설은 심각한 사건이나 문제를 제기하지 않고 그러기에 문제에 대한 해결방안을 제시하지 않는다. 단지 우리가 당면하고 있는 현실을 잔잔한 필치로 그려냄으로써 우리 세대와 이전 세대 그리고 다음 세대의 삶에 대해 생각하게 한다. 변화한 가정의 의미, 가장으로서 아버지가 지고 가는 삶의 무게에 대해서도 생각할 거리를 제공해준다. 무엇보다도 「문 앞에서」는 소심하게 살아온 평범한 아버지들의 모습을 애정을 담아 과장 없이 보여주는 고요하고 담백한 소설이다.

thing in the world is none other than the human, which vividly demonstrates the times his father has lived through, far more perilous and difficult than many individuals have had to endure.

The son, as a young man, deeply resents his father. In the eyes of the young man, his father, who lives his entire life in poverty, is grossly incompetent and unlucky in everything he does. The son in his late forties, however, realizes how much he now resembles his father, which perhaps serves as a catalyst in his later efforts to understand him. Upon meeting his father in an unexpected place and time, he at first sees only his own face in his father's, perhaps, just a bit older and more haggard. Although they have taken different courses in life, the burden of their responsibility and perseverance as the patriarchs of their families, which they have carried on their shoulders throughout their lives, have left their marks on both of their faces. The son realizes how much these marks look alike.

This novel does not depict any serious events or difficult problems and therefore, does not propose any solutions. It only serenely narrates the realities we face, compelling us think about the lives of the people of our own, previous, and the future gen-erations. It also gives us a chance to ponder the changed definition of "home" and the burden of life the father, as the head of a family, alone has to shoulder. Above all, "Outside the Door" is a serene and frank narrative that describes, with affection and without exaggeration, the image of the ordi-nary father who has lived the life of the timid.

비평의 목소리

Critical Acclaim

이동하의 소설은 솜씨 좋은 소목장이 심혈을 기울여 만든 정교한 가구와 같은 느낌을 준다. 빈틈없는 구성, 적확한 어휘 선택, 그 어휘들 가운데 어느 하나도 외따로 놀지 않게 제자리를 찾아 앉히는 정확한 문장 등의 요인 때문이다. 그는 진정한 의미에서의 장인이다.

정호웅

이동하의 소설을 읽으면 그가 얼마나 진하게, 마음속에 뿌리 깊게 인간에 대한 사랑을 지니고 있는 작가인지를 느끼게 된다. 그가 모든 작품을 통해서 말하려고 하는 주제는 결국 사랑으로 귀착된다. 그래서 그의 소

Lee Dong-ha's narratives give their readers an impression that they are looking at a marvelous piece of furniture elaborated by a master cabinet-maker. His meticulous story structure, precise choice in words, compact, forceful sentences that make the most effective use of each and every word—all point to the fact that the writer is an artisan in the truest sense of the word.

Jeong Ho-ung

Reading Lee Dong-ha's stories, one is bound to feel the intense love for humanity that is deeply rooted in the writer's heart. All of the themes the

설은 사랑이 없는 공간, 즉 인간성이 상실된 어떤 상황에서 그것을 지키고자 하는 인물들의 비인간적 상황이 제시되고 있다. 이러한 비인간적인 상황들이 인물들의 인간성을 파괴시킨다. 이것은 이동하의 경험적 인식을 통하여 작품에 형상화되었다. 그의 소설에 등장하는 인물들은 하나같이 힘없고, 슬프고, 외로운 존재들이며, 무기력한 평범한 소시민들이다.

황영숙

「지붕 위의 산책」등 13편의 중단편 소설을 수록한 최근 소설집『문 앞에서』는 이동하의 의도적인 미세서사의 취택 경향을 더욱 잘 보여주고 있다.『문 앞에서』의 수록 작품 가운데는 동시대의 다른 작품들에서 흔히 보이는 1980년대 이후의 역사적 사건을 아주 부분적으로라도 다룬 것을 찾을 수 없다. 사실상, 작가 이동하의 개인사는 미소서사의 취택 경향을 일관되게 보여준 과정이라고 할 수 있다. 거대서사의 필요조건의 하나인 역사적 사건은 그의 소설에서 드물게 그것도 원경(遠景)으로 나타나고 있을 뿐이다.

조남현

writer chooses for his stories boil down to one ultimate subject: love. Lee's main characters are forced into inhuman situations, ironically as a result of their own efforts to safeguard humanity in the middle of loveless spaces, societies suffering from a loss of humanity. In turn, these inhuman situations destroy these characters' humanity. While giving shapes to this irony, the writer draws extensively on his experiential perceptions. All of his protagonists are weak, sad, and lonely beings, powerless, ordinary men of the lower middle class.

Hwang Yeong-suk

The recently published collection, *Outside the Door,* features 13 short and medium-length stories including "A Stroll on the Rooftop," that show, more plainly than ever, Lee Dong-ha's intentional gravitation towards the micro-narratives. None of the stories in this collection deals with, or even hints at, the historical events of the country after the 1980s, which appear frequently in the contemporary works of other authors. In fact, the writer's personal life has everything to do with his inclination to micro-narratives. The historical events, which are one of the requirements for the macro-narratives,

이동하의 소설은 공허와 우수 혹은 의혹과 분노 등 멜랑콜리의 감정이 문화적·역사적 객관성을 구비한 현실임을 암시한다. 그는 현대사를 애도할 수 없는 치명적 상실의 감각, 즉 멜랑콜리의 정서로 담아낸다. 그는 규정할 수도 표상할 수도 명명할 수도 없는 트라우마를 상실의 이름으로 불러내어 실체화하고, 현존하지 않는 그것을 존재의 영역으로 불러내기 위해 다양한 미적 전략을 선보인다. 그의 소설은 간혹 통속적인 보상심리에 이끌리기도 하지만 멜랑콜리를 한국인의 근대적 시간의 의미를 성찰하는, 침통한 지혜로 전략화한다.

김은하

appear in his works only rarely, in the distant background at that.

Lee Dong-ha's novels allude to the fact that the melancholic feelings of emptiness, gloom, suspicion, fury, and so forth are realities grounded in cultural and historical objectivity. He represents the modern history of the nation with a sense of loss, [more precisely, the fatal loss of the ability to mourn] by depicting it in the language of melancholy. He embodies the trauma that is not determinable, representable, or nameable by conjuring it in the name of loss, and uses various aesthetic strategies to bring out the non-existent trauma into the realm of existence. His stories, at times, tend to be drawn to the popular "compensation mentality," but arrange to use melancholy as a source of grave wisdom that may enable us Koreans to reflect on the significance of the nation's modern era.

Kim Eun-ha

이동하

소설가 이동하의 호적 이름은 용(勇)이고, 아명은 윤이다. 그는 1942년 일본 오사카 근처 소읍에서 아버지 이득기와 어머니 김임조 사이의 장남으로 출생한다. 해방이 되자 그의 가족은 고향 경북 경산군 남천면 대명동으로 이사한다. 경산에서 부산 쪽으로 한 정거장 가면 삼성역이 있는데, 그는 삼성면에서 유년 시절을 보낸다. 남천초등학교 1학년에 한국전쟁이 발발한다.

초등학교 3학년 때 휴전이 되고 이듬해에 가족은 고향을 떠나 대구로 이사한다. 이때부터 이동하에게는 지긋지긋한 가난이 따라다닌다. 이후 가난 때문에 남들보다 늦게 학교를 마치게 된다. 대구 서부초등학교 가교사에서 한 학기를 마치고 교회가 운영하는 야학교인 천우성경구락부에서 초등 과정을 마친다. 먹고사는 문제로 학업을 자주 중단하다 대구 칠성동에 있는 칠성중학교를 마친다. 대성고등학교를 남들보다 3, 4년 늦게 졸업한다. 그 시절 끔찍한 가난은 어머니를 앗아갔다. 중학교 시절 국어를 담당하던 이동수 선생님을 만난 것과

Lee Dong-ha

Lee Dong-ha is listed by the name of Yong in his family register and was called Yun as a child. He was born as the eldest son of his father, Lee Deuk-gi and his mother, Kim Im-jo, in a small town near Osaka, Japan in 1942. After Korea was liberated from the Japanese colonial occupation, his family moved to their hometown, Daemyeong-dong, Namchon-myeon, Gyeongsan-gun, Gyeongsang-buk-do in Korea. One train station away from Gyeongsan towards Pusan was Samsong train station; Lee Dong-ha spent his childhood years in Samsong-myeon. When he was a first grader in Namchon Elementary School, the Korean War broke out.

When he was in the third grade at the elementary school, the cease-fire was declared and the next year, his family left their hometown and moved to the city of Daegu. From then on, poverty followed his family doggedly, leading to his delayed elementary education. After attending the temporary schoolhouse of Sobu Elementary School in Daegu

신라예술제 행사의 하나였던 백일장에 참가한 것이 청소년 시절 그에게는 중요한 문학적 자극이었다.

1965년 서울 미아리에 자리잡고 있던 서라벌 예술대학 문예창작학과에 입학한다. 문단의 중진들로 구성된 교수진과 문재를 자랑하던 급우들은 이동하를 주눅들게 했다. 김동리, 서정주, 박목월, 이범선, 김수영, 이형기, 곽종원 등의 강의를 들으며 임영조, 김형영, 박건한, 마종하, 김청, 김정례, 나연숙, 강철수 등과 어울렸다. 대학 시절 그는 초라한 옷차림에 소심하고, 자격지심이 많은 학생이었다. 그러나 이동하는 열등감을 극복하기 위해 더욱 문학에 매달렸다.

1966년은 그에게 중요한 해였다. 몇 개의 문학상을 수상하면서 문학인으로서의 길과 생활인으로서의 길을 간신히 이어갈 수 있었기 때문이다. 대학 1학년이 지나갈 때쯤 《서울신문》 신춘문예에 「전쟁과 다람쥐」가 당선되었고, 같은 해 《현대문학》 장편소설 공모에 『우울한 귀향』이 당선되었다. 여름에는 문화공보부 신인예술상 소설 부문에 「겨울 비둘기」가 수석을 했다. 이후 이동하는 특별히 다작하는 해는 없었지만 쉬는 해도 없이 꾸준한 작품 활동을 이어간다.

for one semester, he moved to an evening church-run school called Chon'u Bible Club, studying there until he graduated. Poverty forced him to attend middle school on and off, but eventually he graduated from Chilseong Middle School in Chilseong-dong, Daegu. By the time he graduated from Dae-seong High School, his contemporaries had already graduated three or four years earlier. At the time, the daily toll of this sort of life took his mother's life. His meeting with Yi Dong-su, who taught Korean in Chilseong Middle School, and his entrance into a writing competition organized for the Silla Art Festival, were crucial literary impetuses in Lee Dong-ha in his adolescence.

In 1965, he entered the Sorabol Art College located in Miari, Seoul and enrolled in the Department of Creative Writing. He felt shy and reserved surrounded by a faculty composed of the prominent writers of the time and a number of talented fellow students. Listening to the lectures given by Kim Dong-ri, Suh Jeong-ju, Park Mok-wol, Lee Beom-seon, Kim Su-yeong, Lee Hyeong-gi, Gwak Jong-won, and so on, he made friends with fellow writers Im Yeong-jo, Kim Hyeong-yeong, Park Geon-han, Ma Jong-ha, Kim Cheong, Kim Jeong-

1970년 전북 정읍 태생의 심옥순과 결혼한다. 1972년
에는 건국대학교 신문사로 직장을 옮겨 1981년까지 다
니면서 동교 대학원 국문과 석사과정을 이수한다. 1978
년 첫 창작집『모래』를, 1979년 두 번째 창작집『바람의
집』을 간행한다. 1970년대 소설가들의 경향은 대중 취
향의 소설을 양산하는 그룹과 민중문학 혹은 실천문학
을 강조하는 그룹으로 나눌 수 있었다. 이동하는 이 시
기 내내 활발한 작품 활동을 했지만 문단의 이러한 두
흐름에는 일정한 거리를 두고 있었다. 그래서인지 이동
하는 평단이나 대중으로부터 큰 관심을 받지 못했다.

1980년대는 이동하에게 생활과 창작 양쪽에서 안정
적이고 생산적이었던 시기였다. 1981년 목포대학교 국
어국문학과의 전임강사로 초빙되어 내려간다. 다음해
「장난감 도시」「굶주린 혼」「유다의 시간」을 엮어 연작
중편집『장난감 도시』를 간행한다. 이 책으로 제1회 한
국문학평론가협회상을 수상한다. 1986년 단편「폭력연
구」「폭력요법」으로 제31회 현대문학상을 수상한다. 같
은 해 세 번째 작품집『저문 골짜기』를 간행한다. 1987
년 네 번째 창작집『폭력연구』를 간행한다. 1989년 다섯
번째 창작집『삼학도』를 간행한다. 이 시기 간행된『장

rye, Na Yeon-suk, and Kang Cheol-su. During his college years, he was a timid and self-reproachful student and was often embarrassed by his state of dress. Nevertheless, Lee Dong-ha immersed himself in literature in order to overcome his various inferiority complexes.

The year 1966 was an important year for Lee Dong-ha. He received several literary awards, which enabled him, if barely, to continue his literary career while earning a living. At the end of his first year in college, his story "War and Squirrel" won the *Seoul Shinmun* Spring Literary Contest, and, later in the same year, *Gloomy Homecoming* won the full-length novel competition sponsored by *Hyundae Munhak* (Contemporary Literature) literary magazine. That summer, "Winter Pigeon" won first prize in the novel category for the New Artist Award competition sponsored by the Ministry of Culture and Public Information. From then on, Lee Dong-ha, while never being particularly prolific, has produced works every year at a steady pace.

In 1970, he married Shim Ok-sun from the Jeongeup, Jeollabuk-do. Two years later, he changed his job and began working for the Konkuk University Newspaper and stayed there until 1981.

난감 도시』와 『폭력연구』는 90년대 『문 앞에서』와 함께 이동하의 대표 작품집으로 꼽힌다.

1991년 3월 중앙대학교 문예창작학과로 직장을 옮긴다. 1992년 중편 「문 앞에서」를 발표한다. 이 무렵 이동하의 소설은 큰 변화를 보여준다. 그는 이전 소설에서 부정적인 모습으로 그리던 아버지를 긍정적으로 그리기 시작한다. 「문 앞에서」에서는 연로하고 나약해진 아버지에 대한 인간적인 연민이 표나게 드러난다. 이동하는 이 소설로 1993년 제1회 오영수문학상을 수상한다. 1997년 「그는 화가 났던가?」를 발표하고 이어 작품집 『문 앞에서』를 간행한다. 이동하는 자신의 소설에 대해 "나에게 나의 소설은 무엇이기를 바라는가? 그것은 못질하기여야 한다. 보다 크고 완전한 것에다 내 작고 불안한 존재를 단단히 못질하고자 하는 노력이어야 한다"고 말한 바 있다. 그의 이러한 못질하기는 문인 모두가 인정하는 그의 성실성으로 지금까지 꾸준히 이어지고 있다.

While working for the newspaper, he completed an M.A. program majoring in Korean literature at the same university. His first collection, *Sand,* was published in 1978 and his second, *The House of the Wind,* in 1979. The literary trends in the 1970s were divided into two camps: one camp more dedicated to the production of volumes of works catering to the public taste and the other that emphasized so-called grassroots literature. Although Lee Dong-ha was actively writing in the period, he kept his distance from both camps. Perhaps, this might explain why he didn't cultivate much popularity from either critics or the general public at the time.

The 1980s marked a stable and productive decade for Lee Dong-ha in both his personal life and literary output. In 1981, he was invited by the Department of Korean Language and Literature at Mokpo University as a full-time lecturer. The next year, he published a novella trilogy *Toy City*, composed of "Toy City," "Starving Soul," and "The Time of Judas." With this trilogy, he received the first Society of Korean Literary Critics Award. In 1986, his "Research on Violence" and "Therapy of Violence" won the 31st Hyundae Literary Award. In the same year, he had his third collection *Valley After Dark* published, followed by his forth collection *Research on Violence* in 1987. The fifth collection came out in 1989 under the title of *Samhak Island*. *Toy City* and *Research on Violence*, along with *Outside the Door* were published in the 1990s, all of which are now considered Lee Dong-ha's most important works.

In March 1991, he shifted his work to the Department of Creative Writing at Chungang University. In 1992, he published the novella *Outside the Door*. With this work as a turning point, Lee Dong-ha's creative world underwent a significant change. The writer began depicting father characters in a positive light unlike earlier. In *Outside the Door,* the narrator's humane compassion for his aged and weakened father is quite evident. With this novel, Lee Dong-ha received the first Oh Yeong-su Literary Award in 1993. In 1997, he published "Was He Angry?" followed by a collection entitled *Outside the Door*. On one occasion, Lee Dong-ha said regarding his novels: "What do I want my novels to mean to me? Each of them is like nailing something down. I want my writing to be like I'm nailing down my small and insecure self onto something larger and more perfect." Lee Dong-ha's "nailing of self" still continues with untiring sincerity today, recognized and admired by all the men of letters.

번역 **전미세리** Translated by Jeon Miseli

한국외국어대학교 동시통역대학원을 졸업한 후, 캐나다 브리티시컬럼비아 대학교 도서관학, 아시아학과 문학 석사, 동 대학 비교문학과 박사 학위를 취득하고 강사 및 아시아 도서관 사서로 근무했다. 한국국제교류재단 장학금을 지원받았고, 캐나다 연방정부 사회인문과학연구회의 연구비를 지원받았다. 오정희의 단편 「직녀」를 번역했으며 그 밖에 서평, 논문 등을 출판했다.

Jeon Miseli is graduate from the Graduate School of Simultaneous Interpretation, Hankuk University of Foreign Studies and received her M.L.S. (School of Library and Archival Science), M.A. (Dept. of Asian Studies) and Ph.D. (Programme of Comparative Literature) at the University of British Columbia, Canada. She taught as an instructor in the Dept. of Asian Studies and worked as a reference librarian at the Asian Library, UBC. She was awarded the Korea Foundation Scholarship for Graduate Students in 2000. Her publications include the translation "Weaver Woman"(*Acta Koreana*, Vol. 6, No. 2, July 2003) from the original short story "Chingnyeo"(1970) written by Oh Jung-hee.

감수 **전승희, 데이비드 윌리엄 홍** Edited by Jeon Seung-hee and David William Hong

전승희는 서울대학교와 하버드대학교에서 영문학과 비교문학으로 박사 학위를 받았으며, 현재 하버드대학교 한국학 연구소의 연구원으로 재식하며 아시아 문예 계간지 《ASIA》 편집위원으로 활동 중이다. 현대 한국문학 및 세계문학을 다룬 논문을 다수 발표했으며, 바흐친의 『장편소설과 민중언어』, 제인 오스틴의 『오만과 편견』 등을 공역했다. 1988년 한국여성연구소의 창립과 《여성과 사회》의 창간에 참여했고, 2002년부터 보스턴 지역 피학대 여성을 위한 단체인 '트랜지션하우스' 운영에 참여해 왔다. 2006년 하버드대학교 한국학 연구소에서 '한국 현대사와 기억'을 주제로 한 워크숍을 주관했다.

Jeon Seung-hee is a member of the Editorial Board of *ASIA*, and a Fellow at the Korea Institute, Harvard University. She received a Ph.D. in English Literature from Seoul National University and a Ph.D. in Comparative Literature from Harvard University. She has presented and published numerous papers on modern Korean and world literature. She is also a co-translator of Mikhail Bakhtin's *Novel and the People's Culture* and Jane Austen's *Pride and Prejudice*. She is a founding member of the Korean Women's Studies Institute and of the biannual Women's Studies' journal *Women and Society* (1988), and she has been working at 'Transition House,' the first and oldest shelter for battered women in New England. She organized a workshop entitled "The Politics of Memory in Modern Korea" at the Korea Institute, Harvard University, in 2006. She also served as an advising committee member for the Asia-Africa Literature Festival in 2007 and for the POSCO Asian Literature Forum in 2008.

데이비드 윌리엄 홍은 미국 일리노이주 시카고에서 태어났다. 일리노이대학교에서 영문학을, 뉴욕대학교에서 영어교육을 공부했다. 지난 2년간 서울에 거주하면서 처음으로 한국인과 아시아계 미국인 문학에 깊이 몰두할 기회를 가졌다. 현재 뉴욕에서 거주하며 강의와 저술 활동을 한다.

David William Hong was born in 1986 in Chicago, Illinois. He studied English Literature at the University of Illinois and English Education at New York University. For the past two years, he lived in Seoul, South Korea, where he was able to immerse himself in Korean and Asian-American literature for the first time. Currently, he lives in New York City, teaching and writing.

바이링궐 에디션 한국 대표 소설 053

문 앞에서

2014년 3월 7일 초판 1쇄 인쇄 | 2014년 3월 14일 초판 1쇄 발행

지은이 이동하 | 옮긴이 전미세리 | 펴낸이 김재범
감수 전승희, 데이비드 윌리엄 홍 | 기획 정은경, 전성태, 이경재
편집 정수인, 이은혜 | 관리 박신영 | 디자인 이춘희
펴낸곳 (주)아시아 | 출판등록 2006년 1월 27일 제406-2006-000004호
주소 서울특별시 동작구 서달로 161-1(흑석동 100-16)
전화 02.821.5055 | 팩스 02.821.5057 | 홈페이지 www.bookasia.org
ISBN 979-11-5662-002-0 (set) | 979-11-5662-010-5 (04810)
값은 뒤표지에 있습니다.

Bi-lingual Edition Modern Korean Literature 053

Outside the Door

Written by Lee Dong-ha | **Translated by** Jeon Miseli
Published by Asia Publishers | 161-1, Seodal-ro, Dongjak-gu, Seoul, Korea
Homepage Address www.bookasia.org | **Tel**. (822).821.5055 | **Fax**. (822).821.5057
First published in Korea by Asia Publishers 2014
ISBN 979-11-5662-002-0 (set) | 979-11-5662-010-5 (04810)

〈바이링궐 에디션 한국 대표 소설〉 작품 목록(1~45)

도서출판 아시아는 지난 반세기 동안 한국에서 나온 가장 중요하고 첨예한 문제의식을 가진 작가들의 작품들을 선별하여 총 105권의 시리즈를 기획하였다. 하버드 한국학 연구원 및 세계 각국의 우수한 번역진들이 참여하여 외국인들이 읽어도 어색함이 느껴지지 않는 손색없는 번역으로 인정받았다. 이 시리즈는 세계인들에게 문학 한류의 지속적인 힘과 가능성을 입증하는 전집이 될 것이다.

바이링궐 에디션 한국 대표 소설 set 1

분단 Division

산업화 Industrialization

여성 Women

바이링궐 에디션 한국 대표 소설 set 2

자유 Liberty